'In the follow-up to his wildly ambitious debut novel, *The Revolutionaries Try Again* (2016), Cárdenas again deploys his sense of invention and irreverence, jettisoning conventional paragraph and dialogue breaks and embracing long-running sentences that delight in playful exasperation... This quirky, playful, difficult novel will appeal to fans of Latin American fiction that navigates the bleeding edge of experimentation.'   *Booklist*

'Buckle up, kids, Cárdenas is taking us on a bumpy ride... *Aphasia* is an avalanche of language, perfect for readers of Thomas Bernhard and Lucy Ellmann's *Ducks, Newburyport.*'   *Book Culture*

'Excellent... *Aphasia*'s spirit is one of blending and border collapse... [It] dramatizes our ability to occupy multiple narratives at once – and proves that literature itself can do the same.'

High Country News

'Thrilling... A writer of originality who makes the English language sound like music.'   *Bookworm* (KCRW)

'Modern, psychological, and very poignant...[*Aphasia*] has made a strong impression on its readers, myself included.'

Sounds and Colours

'Pacy, dense and enlivening... Vividly, colourfully assembled, sensitive to the small contradictions and failings of our lives and histories, *Aphasia* reminds us not so much that we contain multitudes as that multitudes contain us.'   *ABC Arts*, Australia

Praise for *The Revolutionaries Try Again*

'This is an original, insubordinate novel, like his grammar, like his syntax, but fabulously, compellingly readable, with endearing characters.'
New York Times

'A high-octane, high-modernist debut novel from the gifted, fleet Mauro Javier Cárdenas.'
Harper's Magazine

'Exuberant, cacophonous... Cárdenas dizzyingly leaps from character to character, from street protests to swanky soirees, and from lengthy uninterrupted interior monologues to rapid-fire dialogues and freewheeling satirical radio programs, resulting in extended passages of brilliance.'
Publishers Weekly (starred review)

'While [*The Revolutionaries Try Again*] is, indeed, very much a novel rather than a political manifesto – it depicts four childhood friends as they regroup in adulthood and aim to change their country's politics for the better – Cárdenas reveals, via some stunning and shapeshifting prose, that politics in Ecuador isn't as straightforward as it appears on its surface, and very often it amounts to little more than a vain exercise in egobuilding and self-fantasy.'
Kenyon Review

'Cárdenas's gift is to show, through long, brilliant sentences, the charm of inaction and delinquency.'
New Yorker

'Cárdenas's spellbinding book should appeal to McOndo devotees and Bolaño fans alike... A novel that redefines the Latin American identity in a world characterized by social technology and ever-blurring ethnic boundaries.'
Los Angeles Review of Books

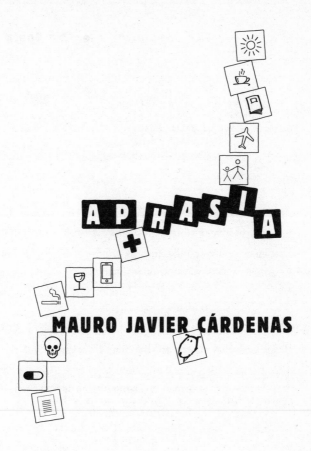

APHASIA

MAURO JAVIER CÁRDENAS

ONEWORLD

A Oneworld Book

First published in Great Britain, the Republic of Ireland and Australia
by Oneworld Publications, 2021
This paperback edition published 2022

ISBN 978-0-86154-128-7
ISBN 978-0-86154-010-5 (eBook)

Printed and bound in Great Britain by Clays Ltd, Elcograf S.p.A

Oneworld Publications
10 Bloomsbury Street
London WC1B 3SR
England

CONTENTS

S 8

WHEN ANTONIO WAS ARTURO

Once again his daughters and his former wife packed their lives and left him to summer in Czechia with Babička and Děda, and unlike the previous seven summers, Antonio wasn't anxious for them to leave already so he could sleep with former girlfriends or new girlfriends or whomever he happened to meet at bookstores or nightclubs or on the internet, on the contrary, he was anxious that they were leaving him because on the one hand he didn't want to be without them (Ada, his eight-year-old, was becoming an ace on the soccer field, and Eva, his five-year-old, was already tinkering with the upright piano he'd abandoned years ago), and on the other hand he'd resigned himself to a so-called stable family life in Los Angeles alongside his former wife due to his daughters, so he didn't want to be alone and risk chancing upon any more women like Dora (philosophy major, S3) or Silvina (science fiction writer, S7) who might remind him of the other lives he could have lived if he'd left his former wife when he was planning to, three weeks before conceiving Ada and three months before he was asked by her parents to marry her, and although one never really knows why one does what one does—at least I like to believe I don't always know, Antonio writes, so as to feel less programmed by the catastrophes of my childhood—it is likely that his desire to avoid chancing upon any more women like Dora or Silvina who might rattle the family arrangement that was allowing his daughters to bloom beautifully was what led him, on summer #8, to join a website called Your Sugar Arrangements for $69.99 a month.

—

An internet executive overdoses on heroin and his companion doesn't phone the paramedics but instead leaves him to die on his yacht, the internet reports, a companion with a history of not phoning the paramedics in similar circumstances and whom the internet executive met through a website called Your Sugar Arrangements, which is how Antonio first heard of Your Sugar Arrangements: what in the world is this website, Antonio remembers thinking, and since he doesn't inject himself with heroin and can't isolate himself dangerously inside a yacht — I have no interest in yachts, Antonio writes, or people who frequent yachts — on one of his first evenings alone on summer #8, as he was waiting for a stool at Salt Air, he angled his phone so no one could see him browsing a site called Your Sugar Arrangements (YSA), typing Arturo Ventanas as his username and joining this website out of curiosity, he told himself, not expecting to become a Sugar Daddy (SD) to any Sugar Baby (SB), as advertised on the website, nor expecting to become another successful male looking to fuel mutually beneficial, no-strings-attached (NSA) relationships with beautiful young women, as also advertised on the website, although financially he'd done okay enough to maybe belong to the Practical designation in the SB allowance section called Expectation / Budget ($1,000 to $3,000 monthly), as opposed to the High (more than $10,000 monthly), although he selected Negotiable (openly negotiable to any amount) because in the past he'd experienced bouts of nihilist spending (mostly on clothes from Saint Laurent) so he didn't want to rule out the possibility of throwing away his database analyst salary on these new types of arrangements.

—

One day you're at Saint Ignatius Catholic Church marrying someone because she's expecting your child, one day you're at the same church listening to Schubert's Piano Trio No. 2 in E-Flat during your lunch hour, one day the young pianist who performed in that Schubert Trio is unbuttoning your jeans at the Pelican Yacht Harbor in Sausalito: her YSA name is Jasmine and she claimed to be a classical pianist who was studying at the Curtis Institute of Music, a claim that, unlike the many other claims on the many other profiles he has been encountering on Your Sugar Arrangements, turned out to be true, and perhaps because she already knew about the excess of falsehoods on Your Sugar Arrangements, she messaged him that she was performing at Saint Ignatius Catholic Church, so there he was in the audience during his lunch hour, two days before he was to meet her in person for the first time, sitting in the pews amidst the Catholic paraphernalia of his youth and at least a hundred retirees who seemed to believe they were entitled to free classical music during their lunch hour and at the same time seemed to be performing the joyousness of being alive, isn't this incredible, Gertrude, at last we have time to listen to this beautiful music, the nineteenth-century music Antonio used to fumble when he was twenty-one and learning to play the piano, the tempestuous music of Chopin and Rachmaninoff that he later rejected as tonal kitsch, the Schubert Piano Trio No. 2 in E-Flat that he is listening to now as he runs SQL queries at Prudential Investments, remembering that afternoon a few weeks ago at Saint Ignatius Catholic Church, sitting in the pews and feeling like he'd been invited to participate in a public game of foreplay, yes, Arturo, you will watch me rousing the retirees with my pianistic vitality, and you will not talk to me after my performance, not yet, you will just watch me bow to the audience of the elderly, I won't even know if you're in the audience, but please don't imagine you're at one of those peep shows your hairdresser told you about, the kind where you insert a handful of coins to see me behind a glass pane because we're in church, for god's sake, and a decrepit priest just announced the afternoon program, and a beautiful woman in the balcony is about to film me from the wrong angle, yes, Arturo, that's my mother and she has at least two rich boyfriends right now and she's about your age, although you will never tell me your real age is thirty-nine, just as you will never tell me that one day you were at Saint Ignatius Catholic Church about to marry someone because she was expecting your child, or that nine years later, when you showed up to see me at Saint Ignatius, you didn't feel any longing or regret or any of the strong emotions associated with returning to the church where you married someone because she was expecting your child, no, you were simply listening to my rendition of the Schubert Piano Trio No. 2 in E-Flat, enjoying the wonders of being alive just like the one hundred and one retirees around you, isn't this incredible, Arturo, and that evening you will message me and tell me you were in the audience and praise me and tell me you recognized the cellist I was playing with from a performance of Steve Reich's Cello Counterpoint at Carnegie Hall, and two days later I will cancel on you minutes before our dinner at Salt Air because I panicked about you knowing my real identity—I didn't want to mix up my life in YSA with my real life, Arturo, Jasmine messaged him later—and despite your messages reassuring me that you also had an incentive to be discreet—I deleted your voicemails, Jasmine said a few days later, I was scared to listen to them—I didn't change my mind until later that night, after you sent me a link to your publications, although I had already done a search on you to verify you weren't a criminal, and three days after Jasmine canceled their first dinner at Salt Air, the game of public foreplay continued in the Bay

Area, during dinner at Sushi Ran in Sausalito, where Arturo and Jasmine engaged in a heated conversation about John Cage, Chopin, etc., trying to impress each other without touching each other just yet—I don't know why I canceled on you or why I later changed my mind, Jasmine messaged him later, I don't think we make decisions like these logically, I had a gut feeling that something terrible was going to happen during dinner, that's all, I just didn't think you could possibly know so much about classical music, everyone in YSA exaggerates themselves 150 percent, everyone is tall and handsome and then they turn out to be bald businessmen or scrawny tech people—I just remembered another reason I originally didn't want to meet you, Jasmine messaged him later, you told me you were a novelist, so I immediately assumed you'd be one of those cynical emo pretentious types who would tell me how depressing the world was, I don't know why I remembered that just now as I was practicing my scales—and after dinner at Sushi Ran, Jasmine said let's stroll to the pier, so they strolled arm in arm to the dark pier and stepped down to the empty Pelican Yacht Harbor, joking that in movies something terrible always happens in these kinds of harbors, and when they reached the end of the harbor she approached him and kissed him, and he unzipped her white jeans and discovered she was not faking her arousal, and she unbuttoned his black jeans and discovered he was not faking his arousal, and he wondered whether the knees of her white jeans would be soiled by the damp floorboards such that later her mother would be able to guess what her nineteen-year-old daughter had been up to, and he looked around at the dark sea and the vacant yachts and thought life is unbelievable and beautiful, there's even a discarded bench cushion Jasmine can repurpose to lie down, and then it was over and she didn't ask him for an allowance and he walked her back to her mother's 1980s BMW and she was gone.

WHEN ANTONIO WAS NICOLA

To be Nicola, Antonio thinks, to ride his Shadow VLX, far, to the Nuart Theatre, toward the traffic of 405, to be Nicola instead of Antonio just as Nicola's brother, Matteo, had wanted to be Nicola, to tell his former wife, when she was eight and a half months pregnant with Ada, and his mother, who was visiting for Christmas, that he had to leave them for six hours to watch The Best of Youth at the Nuart Theatre, three hours of Nicola Carati and his family on Saturday afternoon, three more hours on Sunday evening—if you're feeling strong enough, Nicola says to his daughter, drive to your mother—to ride to the Nuart Theatre on a motorcycle that rattles him if he crosses the sixty-miles-per-hour mark, to answer dismissively when his former wife and his mother ask him why he needs to watch such a long movie now, can't you wait, his mother said, any minute now your daughter will be born, to not know why he felt the urge to see Best of Youth, no, Antonio thinks, even then he must have known he was riding to the Nuart Theatre to see Best of Youth because Dr. Adler had told him to (because Dr. Adler knew he wanted to become a writer, knew his misgivings about being a father, his dread about being a husband, even knew his dreams because she encouraged him to write them down and share them with her—I knew a woman who knew my dreams, Antonio writes—and when small birds sighed, Theodore Roethke says, she would sigh back at them—did you agree to become a father to please Dr. Adler?—does it matter now?—dear Dr. Adler, Antonio writes, thank you for the new family you've given me—an Italian movie like a Tolstoy novel, Dr. Adler said—), to know why he felt the urge to see Best of Youth but to not know how to explain this urge to his former wife or his mother, but perhaps Dr. Adler, who used to believe and perhaps still believes that only the interaction between doctor and patient changes the patient, in other words only in the warmth of Dr. Adler's office could Antonio rehearse how to be other than what he was, told him to watch Best of Youth not for literary reasons but because she wanted him to learn how to be Nicola, as he has indeed tried to do, watching Best of Youth so many times over the years that he has come to believe he can speak Italian like Nicola—voltate!—to learn how to be a father from a movie might sound ridiculous, Antonio writes, but how else do men learn to be fathers different from their own monstrous fathers?—holotropic breathwork?—tried it once already—constellation therapy?—twice—okay you're excused, be Nicola—to be Nicola, who plays limbo with his young daughter late into the night, who playacts at being Charlie Chaplin to amuse his young daughter, who, after his wife leaves him to join the Red Brigades, rearranges his life so he can spend most of his time with his young daughter and never remarries just as Antonio's mother never remarried while Antonio and his sister lived with her—your daughter has softened you, Nicola's sister says—yes, Antonio writes, that's what daughters do—and one day Nicola's daughter, who despite being abandoned by her mother has become a lighthearted adult—children are more resilient than we think, Nicola says—receives a letter from her mother, who's finally out of jail, and Nicola's daughter asks Nicola what she should do, and Nicola says if you're feeling strong enough, drive to your mother, and so she does, waiting for her mother with a bouquet of flowers outside the library where her parents met—Mama—embracing her mother—you tried to overthrow the government and now you have to ask permission to play music for me, Nicola's daughter says to her mother inside a church in Florence—to be Nicola's daughter listening to her mother performing Bach on the church organ for her for the first time—Bach's Invention No. 2 in C-Minor, Antonio writes, which I have played for my daughters, too—contemplating the vast universe of those years without her mother—everyone in your dreams is you, Dr. Adler said—Mama—but no, unlike Nicola's daughter, Antonio hadn't been feeling strong enough to board a plane to Baltimore to help his mother handle his sister, who couldn't discern what was / wasn't imaginary anymore, or yes, perhaps he thought he could pretend he was as strong as Nicola's daughter because he had a steady database analyst job at Prudential Investments, two daughters and a former wife who tolerated his erratic attempts to remain with them, so about twelve months ago, a few days after Antonio's mother called him and told him his sister had accused her plus Obama of conspiring against her and had thrown her out of the house she owned in Baltimore (for years Antonio didn't care about houses or cars or whatever else people purchase to pass the time before they die—the pitiful concerns of philistines, I probably thought back then, Antonio writes—and so for years Antonio ignored his sister whenever she asked him to please bring his daughters to her new house in Baltimore, a house his mother often talked about not because it was a luxurious home that stood as a symbol of his sister's success in life, but because she knew that house was a comfort to his sister, who had rejected almost everyone in the family as retribution for what she perceived as their rejection of her—a house was a comfort to her, Antonio's mother said, a place of her own—but unfortunately one evening one of his sister's neighbors had parked her car in front of her house, waiting to pick up her kids at the bus stop, and his sister, thinking her neighbor was conspiring against her, had allegedly threatened to shoot her neighbor and the other families at the bus stop if they didn't get off her property, for which she was arrested and charged with multiple counts of assault and cruelty to children—Ms. Marta Terranova stated that Estela Jiménez came to her car and started beating on the window with a knife, the police report says, to the point that one of her children begged Terranova to drive away because she didn't want to die—and so Antonio's mother was concerned that his sister, alone and unsupervised, would aggravate her unfortunate legal situation as she awaited her trial proceedings), Antonio surprised himself by boarding a plane to Baltimore, renting a compact economy car, and driving from the airport to his sister's house, unannounced, of course, armed with the disastrous resolve of the reasonable, no, Antonio thinks, he doesn't want to think about his sister ranting at him about radial frequencies from satellites with lasers, or about his sister throwing him out of her house, or about him and his mother in a government agency filling out forms to commit his sister to a mental institute, so much of that trip to Baltimore he has already forgotten anyway and if he were to think about it too much his mind would be less likely to erase it—I don't intend to write about my sister here, Antonio writes, among my so-called sugar arrangements—nor do I want to give you the impression my so-called sugar arrangements are a diversion from thinking about my sister's misfortunes, Antonio writes, because of course my so-called sugar arrangements are a diversion, but so are all other activities that allow me to pass the time without thinking of the misfortunes that have happened and are still happening to my sister—and although of course Antonio's ashamed of his avoidance, no one needs to know, he won't tell anyone, and thankfully he no longer believes in a god that can strike him for avoiding his sister's misfortunes, so yes, Antonio will rather think about Jasmine from Your Sugar Arrangements, or he'll rather reread A Lexicon of Terror & Other Stories by his last former girlfriend, the science fiction writer he still likes to call Silvina (S7), or transcribe the conversation he recently had with Dora (S3), another former girl-friend, whom Antonio hadn't seen in almost five years, since around the time his second daughter was born (Dora had de-manded that he stop sending her sporadic messages, however seemingly innocuous they might be, resorting to the hackneyed language of breakups to do so—it is disrespectful of you to con-tinue doing so not only to me but to my boyfriend, Dora wrote, and since we're living together he is well aware of any and all efforts you've made—so he hadn't had any contact with her through any medium in those five years, until recently, when he discovered through casual Facebook research that her new rela-tionship had ended since she'd posted a public picture of Bailey, her dog, along with a comment about how her new former boy-friend had stolen her dog and could someone please talk some sense into him—I was not surprised their relationship had ended, Antonio writes, I knew their day would come because it comes to all of us—and so after exchanging seemingly innocuous Face-book messages during the spring, Dora agreed to meet him on a Sunday afternoon outside of Menotti's Coffee Stop in Venice Beach toward the beginning of summer #8), or he'll rather think about his upcoming arrangements this week and the next, or about anything other than his sister's unreason, or her misfortunes due to her unreason, or the accretion of misfortunes that culminated in her unreason, or her whereabouts since she ran away from her trial proceedings in Baltimore a few weeks ago.

DORA & HER DOG BY ANTONIO JOSE JIMÉNEZ

What would you endure jail for, Dora said, I would endure jail for my daughters, Antonio said, I'm not telling you this so you think I'm a good person, father, etc., this is simply the first answer that comes to mind, and because Dora withheld her response for too long, and because he knew she might not offer him another audience, Antonio continued, speaking to her of I've Loved You So Long, a French movie they'd seen together in which a mother endures jail for killing her son (the revelation toward the end of the movie that the mother knew that her son was dying, and that she had injected her boy to spare him because she was a doctor and knew how painful his terminal illness would be, had been so unbearable to Antonio that he had to rush to the bathroom of the Nuart Theatre to conceal his sobbing from Dora—in my own so-called fiction I skirt the verb to sob because of its melodramatic acoustics, Antonio writes, nevertheless to weep aloud with convulsive gasping was what I did at the Nuart Theatre—), I think jail in that movie is the mother's equivalent of killing herself, Antonio said, the question has been on my mind because I did go to jail, Dora said, because apparently her new former boyfriend had gifted her a dog, a dachshund she was carrying with her that Sunday outside of Menotti's Coffee Stop on one of those BabyBjörn carriers that are popular in Abbot Kinney among fathers who want to showcase to the world that they, unlike their own fathers, are good fathers, keeping their newborns close to their chests, after I ended the relationship we enrolled in couples therapy to mediate custody of our dog, Dora said, I'm going to need most of your cigarettes to hear this story about you and your dog,

Antonio said, last winter he traveled to Miami with Bailey and did not return him, Dora said, so she filed charges in small-claims court, won, but apparently the judge didn't have the jurisdiction to issue an injunction for her new former boyfriend to return her dog, I called the police anyway, Dora said, but the police informed her they couldn't enter his house without a court order so she put up flyers with pictures of her dog and of her new former boyfriend in the neighborhood in Manhattan Beach where she used to live with him and her dog, did you tape or hammer your flyers to the telephone poles there, Antonio said, why are you asking me these questions are you going to write about this, Dora said, the story of you and your dog is compelling to me because it externalizes what during breakups often remains, against one's will, internalized, Antonio said, elaborating his point by recounting a story by Charles D'Ambrosio in which a screenwriter at an insane asylum asks a ballerina at the same insane asylum why she burns herself with cigarettes, because it externalizes her pain, the ballerina says, I actually handed out most of the flyers, Dora said.

—

The expectation of unconditional love should be reserved for the relationship between parents and children, Antonio said, because it's unreasonable to expect adults to burden one another with unconditional love, and since Dora did not reply Antonio continued, telling her that after he was surprised by the news that he was going to be what he never wanted to be, a father, his former therapist said that one of the most wonderful aspects of being a parent was that you could love someone without worrying about them leaving you, that is absolutely not true, Dora said, children do leave their parents—I knew what she meant, Antonio writes, so I didn't attempt to amuse her with insouciant counterarguments—and perhaps because Dora used to complain he purposefully excluded his life as a father from their relationship, which lasted almost a year, he softened his tone and told her how in his life now he pined after Saturday afternoons, when Ada has her soccer matches, and that to watch Ada score three or four goals per game was beautiful to him, as if he was watching an apparition of himself as a boy playing soccer in Bogotá but much better, although he didn't connect Ada and himself across time until his mother visited and said she's just like you, Antonio, running furiously after the ball—Ada, Antonio writes, my sensitive eight-year-old who paints I'm Sorry canvases for her mother when she splashes too much bathtub water—I am still seeking that kind of unconditional love, Dora said, admitting this probably made her a romantic, it does, Antonio said, but there's nothing right or wrong about being a romantic.

—

Someone called me about my dog, Dora said, was it a man or a woman, Antonio said, guessing it had to be a woman because only a woman would understand the plight of another woman in search of her dog, or at least that's what Antonio thought at the time, sitting next to Dora and her dog outside Menotti's Coffee Stop, a woman, Dora said, a store owner who had seen her dog with a blond woman who happened to be the new girlfriend of Dora's new former boyfriend, that just proves how benighted he is because white girls are the worst and they age horribly, Antonio said, I drove by the store owned by the woman who had called me about my dog, Dora said, what kind of store was it, Antonio said, I'm not telling, Dora said, but I found my dog nearby and snatched it from her, how did you manage to snatch your dog away from the blond woman, Antonio said, for legal reasons I can't tell you too many details, Dora said, did the blond woman chase after you, Antonio said, no, Dora said, the blond woman did not—Dora didn't tell me if the blond woman was already pregnant when she snatched her dog from her, Antonio writes, but the blond woman was pregnant—I'm glad I didn't have children with him, Dora said, obviously the blond woman didn't love your dog enough to chase you and therefore did not deserve to keep your dog, Antonio said, he filed charges against me, Dora said, assault and theft, she didn't think the charges would go through, months passed and nothing happened, but then they did go through and she had to hire a criminal attorney and place her dog in a witness protection program, I've heard of dog therapists and dog dentists so I guess a dog witness protection program isn't too far-fetched, Antonio said, that's just what I called me hiding Bailey outside of California, Dora said.

—

One night at the apartment Dora was sharing with her sister and her brother, a night Antonio would prefer not to forget, Dora shared with him the video her soon-to-be-new father had recorded of her, her two siblings, her soon-to-be-former mother, and her soon-to-be-new mother, all of them in what looked like a train station in Beijing at the moment the adoption transaction was taking place, her brother pretending to be delighted, her older sister as enraged as she was when Antonio met her years later, little Dora smiling in confusion about what was happening to her, her new father recording a video that years later he was to share at a family gathering as a tribute for Dora's former mother, whom he was to bring back from Beijing to marry soon after leaving Dora's new mother—Dora's family history is more complicated than I or anyone can even attempt to reconcile, Antonio writes, and to this day I would not wish it on anyone—enough, Antonio thinks, closing the file entitled Dora & Her Dog and scanning the messages that have been arriving since he began writing about Dora two hours ago, at 7:00 a.m., messages that contain words like autoregressive forecasting, intraday transaction posting, we are now accepting submissions for our Nature issue, the principal assumption of the geometric distributed lag model (GDL) is that the maximum impact of marketing occurs in the period in which it takes place and that its influence declines geometrically to zero thereafter, your suboptimal SQL query is slowing down the Teradata box, pursuant to the terms of the Bail Bond contract and promissory note you agreed to indemnify Any Day Bail Bonding Inc. against any and all claims incurred due to Estela Jiménez's failure to appear in Baltimore's Superior Court you are hereby given ten days to pay $110,000 for failure to appear, attorney fees, interest, and recovery expenses, and as Antonio removes his headphones, which have been transmitting Eight Lines by Steve Reich on repeat, he hears his work phone ringing inside his cubicle at Prudential Investments, Ron Graebel here, Ron Graebel says, I'm the owner of Any Day Bail Bonding I just sent you an email how are you today, you shouldn't call this phone I need to, give me a minute I'll call you from a conference room, Antonio says as he hurries toward Bermuda, the conference room without windows so that no one in the office can see him, okay, Antonio says, I hate making these calls, Ron Graebel says, you have a business to run I understand, Antonio says, do you know your sister's whereabouts, Ron Graebel says, no I, Antonio says, no, you and your mother are responsible for her I know you know that, Ron Graebel says, my mother and I, Antonio says, my sister isn't well she hasn't talked to us in a year, as owner and the one directly responsible to pay the court I would feel a lot better about this case if you would submit the full bond amount to be held in our security deposit account to cover the liability or at a minimum proof of funds, Ron Graebel says, we reserved Bermuda for 9:00 are you almost done, Antonio's coworker says, I'm done I'll call you back, Antonio says, I do expect you will, Ron Graebel says.

—

Aside from finishing law school I'm acting now, Dora said—Dora, Antonio writes, the least expressive woman I've met—she had discovered acting was her calling and acting is about portraying our reactions to dramatic circumstances, life and death, just like in fiction, and Antonio disagreed and said that he subscribed to António Lobo Antunes's belief that we should remove the dramatic charge from fiction because nothing's really that dramatic, someone is always leaving us or dying or going to the insane asylum, these miseries just happen to us and will continue to happen to us, to which she replied by speaking of metaphorical icebergs, the surface of things, etc., but Antonio did not refute these handed-down notions of narrative because he wanted to be amenable so she would agree to a handful of Fridays with him during summer #8, I've changed, Dora said, explaining that her former therapist had encouraged her not to be so black-and-white, to be more comfortable with the gray aspects of life, which included seeing Antonio again, and Antonio said I am Dora's gray area, but Dora didn't laugh, I have begun to see myself again as I was as a three-year-old, Dora said, so open and cheerful, ambling with her new father to the neighborhood ice cream shop, it's remarkable to see oneself as a three-year-old again, Antonio said, across twenty-seven years of life, I would do things differently now, Dora said, and Antonio interpreted this as a reference to her cruelty after she ended their relationship, a topic Antonio had no interest in pursuing (what good would it do now?—besides, Antonio writes, cruelty is embedded in the structure of endings—the day after Dora ended their relationship, Antonio revealed to her, despite his distaste for the hackneyed language of so-called love, that he loved her—I did not conceal my sobbing from her, Antonio writes, and she was taken aback because while we were together she hadn't known—I love you too, she said, but it's too late, she was already seeing the older man who was to steal her dog—just last summer I heard the same response to my untimely revelation of so-called love from Silvina, Antonio writes, the other former girlfriend I wish I could have kept—), if I have learned anything about breakups, Antonio said, and I haven't really learned anything about breakups, and here she interrupted him and said why do you always qualify yourself like that, and he said because I believe this business of learning is a mirage we impose on ourselves to feel better about our fated lives, does that include what I just said about changing, Dora said, that wasn't my intention but yes, Antonio said, reaching across the table to rest his hand on her forearm, wanting her to believe he could believe she could change, why shouldn't we nurse our delusions, Antonio said, if we find consolation in them?

—

I thought it through, Dora said, all the possible angles, whether I was in the wrong and should let Bailey go, or whether I was willing to abide by my principles and endure jail for what truly matters to me, and since Antonio remained quiet she continued, telling him a friend of her new former boyfriend had contacted her and told her that her new former boyfriend was enjoying himself with this business of the dog, getting even with her through her dog, how did his friend know about her dog, Antonio said, I emailed his friends and coworkers, she said, pleading with them about her dog, and as Dora removed her baseball cap to rearrange her hair, Antonio could see what looked like scabs on her forehead and the excessive makeup she had applied to cover them—in my own so-called fiction I don't provide descriptions of people because I don't remember what people look like, Antonio writes, but I remember Dora's forehead because I became concerned Dora wasn't well—she must have intuited that he was considering whether she'd derailed aspects of her mind as a consequence of spending a year plotting the recovery of her dog because she changed the topic and asked him about his relationship status—no way I'm risking a summer affair with Dora, being what I was thinking, Antonio writes—and so Antonio spoke to her about his child custody proceedings and how he had to attend a mandatory orientation where a man described how he had to enter a special building from one door, and how the mother of his child had to enter the same special building through another door, on the other side of the building, and how the man was only allowed to see his son in a special room inside that special building for a limited number of hours—I dream of that building often, Antonio writes, or perhaps I no longer dream of that building and it has simply become one of the images I have to contend with, in other words it is my building now, a building shaped like the Pentagon or the doomed fortresses of Jacques Austerlitz—he spoke to Dora about resignation and how his daughters need a lot of attention, and how he has come to define happiness collectively, and that it was ridiculous, given that most adult relationships end anyway, to pursue a relationship with another adult at the expense of his daughters, who were so little still—I thought I knew the effect my monologue would have on Dora, Antonio writes, the narrative of self-sacrifice, etc., but we were both wearing sunglasses, so I couldn't tell how she was feeling, although even if she hadn't been wearing sunglasses I wouldn't have known how she was feeling—I think your mother giving you away for adoption so you wouldn't die of hunger after your father died in a motorcycle accident is your mother's equivalent of killing herself, Antonio didn't say.

—

I had to turn myself in, Dora said, trying to lighten up her anecdote about jail by saying that she had tried to turn herself in on a day the computer registration systems were down, so she decided to come back another day because if the systems were down she wouldn't know when she was getting out, now would she, I was in jail for one night, Dora said, what was jail like, Antonio said, apparently where you first sit gives away whether or not you've been in jail before, Dora said, and because Antonio didn't want to think about or share with Dora how a year ago his sister had also been in jail after threatening to shoot her neighbors, he asked Dora if walking her dog had become stressful to her, in other words was she worried about running into her new former boyfriend or his future former girlfriend, no, Dora said, showing him her dog's new, difficult-to-snatch harness, I knew I would have to live with this new burden of worry before deciding to snatch my dog from that woman, Dora said, plus she also knew her new former boyfriend was still in Miami, and as Dora and Antonio watched the sun come down outside of Menotti's Coffee Stop—in my so-called fiction I never describe landscapes or weather, suns coming up or going down, Antonio writes, what's the point? everything's searchable online and metaphorical weathers are a bore, but that Sunday the sun was coming down and I didn't know how I was feeling about seeing Dora again—Antonio said this is my favorite time of day, things coming to an end, and since Antonio didn't want her to think he was being metaphorical about endings, he mentioned that these particular colors of sundown reminded him of sundown at Burning Man, a weeklong party in the desert he used to attend when he was in his twenties, speaking to her of people standing atop RVs, the sense of anticipation, the biggest party of their lives about to begin, the fluorescent lights on art cars and the wonderland castles about to be animated by portable generators, and because Dora wasn't smiling he said next time I will add puppetry to my Burning Man story to amuse you better, and Dora said what makes you think I'm not amused?

—

In retrospect I have assumed she didn't want me to leave just yet because she had suggested we walk her dog along the beach toward Santa Monica, Antonio writes, but unfortunately I had to go because my oldest daughter Ada had taken money from her mother without asking and upon being caught had cried for almost two hours, afraid of what I would say to her, I don't want to make Ada wait any longer, I said, I'm also worried about handing out a fair punishment, a lesson about consequences, I explained to Dora, without getting too upset at Ada, and yet Dora seemed upset that I was done with her and her dog, hugging me politely, sideways because of the dog on her chest, our torsos barely touching, kissing each other's cheeks too quickly, letting her dog lick me and playacting at licking him back, neither of us saying let's meet again soon, awakening, later that night, at least three or four times, worried that the excessive smoking I'd done with Dora might have corroded my new tooth implant, ambling, the next morning, from the extra-small studio apartment my daughters call The Other Home, across the laundry room that connects my building with their building, to the apartment where I used to live with my former wife and my two daughters, who were almost done packing for their annual summer trip to Czechia—my former wife and I have nothing in common besides our daughters and perhaps a proclivity for buffoonery, Antonio writes, so our relationship should have ended before we conceived Ada and it has, many times, including a divorce proceeding that led me to write to an acquaintance dear John, thank you for your invitation to join your book club but my life has been reduced to four-way settlement meetings in which a family attorney lectures me about the deleterious impact of pizza on my daughter so he can assign an additional $25 to my former wife's spousal support, but stay tuned, even Moses Herzog recovered — my former wife has tried to date others and I have tried to date others but we both want to see Ada and Eva every day, Antonio writes, so we're not dating anybody anymore — last week my former wife bought me a bookshelf so I wouldn't have to lug my books between Home and The Other Home but didn't tell me it was for me so she was upset I hadn't remarked on it, Antonio writes — I bought you a beautiful bookshelf and you don't say anything, Ida said — perhaps that's the only way adult relationships can last, Antonio writes, by exhaustion, although I wouldn't take relationship advice from me.

WHEN ANTONIO WAS A DATABASE ANALYST

Or perhaps nature no longer exists for me because of my job, Antonio thinks, all these years at Prudential Investments running SQL queries and at the same time not at Prudential Investments running SQL queries, pretending I am not running SQL queries eight hours a day inside a cubicle in the financial district of Los Angeles, I am not here, no, I am at my Jesuit high school in Bogotá praying to our Madre Dolorosa and sprinting after a soccer ball across a barren field that will never see grass (for the last twelve years he has been writing about his Jesuit school years in Bogotá inside a cubicle in the early morning, before beginning his eight hours of SQL queries at 9:00 a.m., and because on the other side of his cubicle wall a product manager has been spending her early morning hours arguing about financial health features on conferences calls with technology managers in multiple time zones, he has had to train himself to write about his Jesuit school years in Bogotá with music set to the highest volume, the same Arvo Pärt / Olivier Messiaen playlist on repeat every day for the last twelve years, which has been transmitted to his ears through oversized circumaural Sennheiser headphones whose headband cracks in the middle after a year or two such that the file cabinet inside his cubicle has become a junkyard of cracked oversized circumaural Sennheiser headphones as well as of obsolete electronics like PalmPilots, Nokias, BlackBerries encrypted by Prudential Investments, all of them stashed inside their sturdy laminated boxes containing limited warranties printed in microscript by Robert Walser, and in that junkyard of a file cabinet you can also find a decade of Antonio's 1040 tax returns, birth certificates for both of his daughters, a bail bond contract assuming obligation for his sister, who due to an accretion of misfortunes he'd rather not think about has been hearing conspirative voices incognizant of the spatiotemporal regulations in the USA, signed documents committing most of his database analyst income to his former wife according to rules set by a mean-spirited divorce attorney), such that, in the early morning, before beginning his eight hours of SQL queries, he has been simultaneously existing in Bogotá, in the alien musical landscapes of Arvo Pärt / Olivier Messiaen, and (not) inside a cubicle in the financial district of Los Angeles, and perhaps this accretion of pretending he isn't where he is has disrupted too many of the pathways inside his brain accountable for his relationship to nature, window after window into nature shuttered by a decision-management hub inside his brain that he hasn't imagined in terms of pathways or operational linkages or tentacles connecting and disconnecting themselves to artifacts from nature like palm trees or cordilleras or panoramas abloom with inspiriting vegetation but in vaguer terms than that, thinking instead of the garbological assemblages he'd seen years ago at an exhibit called The Alternative Guide to the Universe, which, because he barely remembers the details of that exhibit, he has to search online as he considers writing about his (non) relationship to nature inside his cubicle in the financial district of Los Angeles instead of thinking about his sister, yes, there it is, The Alternative Guide to the Universe at the Hayward Gallery in London (he'd actually purchased The Alternative Guide to the Universe catalogue that came with that exhibit, a catalogue that contains essays about fringe physics, symbolic devices, the symbiosis between magic and technology, and one about counternarrative by Antonio's former fiction-writing teacher, who almost ten years ago at the New York State Summer Writers Institute had wondered why Antonio didn't write in Spanish instead of in English, advising him against writing sentences that seemed to contain two or more sentences from two or more narratives at once—pues ya ve que no he cambiado en nada, profe—), and later that evening, after concluding his eight hours of SQL queries, he searches through his The Alternative Guide to the Universe catalogue and finds that the artist responsible for the vague garbological assemblages Antonio has been associating with the decision-management hub that has shuttered his windows into nature is called Richard Greaves, who apparently studied theology and hotel management and quit his job to dedicate himself to assembling his own asymmetrical visions of the world out of abandoned barns, coffeemakers, nicked shovels, computer keyboards, old razors, twine, rope—a nail stops the evolution, Richard Greaves says, but a rope is patient—parsing discarded objects in the forests of Quebec based on his nebulous linkages to them, Antonio writes—and as Antonio marvels at how what seemed like an incondite associative thread turned out to be quite pertinent to his reflections about his (non) relationship to nature, he imagines Richard Greaves spreading his cargo of trash on a kitchen table, trying to find linkages between gnarled tricycles, giant tacks, newsletters about toolboxes, recognizing that this image of Richard Greaves has its origins in Vertigo by W. G. Sebald (and here Antonio searches online inside Vertigo for the word table and finds the passage that according to him describes his own method of composition—I sat at a table near the open terrace door, W. G. Sebald writes, my papers and notes spread out around me, drawing connections between events that lay far apart but which seemed to me to be of the same order—), and yet unfortunately for Antonio the catalogue for The Alternative Guide to the Universe only contains five photographs of Richard Greaves's houses or huts or installations or anarchitectural visions or whatever one wishes to call them—buildings on the verge of disintegration, Valérie Rousseau calls them in The Alternative Guide to the Universe catalogue—and so Antonio orders a book called Richard Greaves Anarchitecte, thinking that if he can spend a few hours contemplating more photographs of Richard Greaves's installations he would be able to construct more compelling visions of the decision-management hub that has shuttered his windows into nature, meanwhile, as he waits for Richard Greaves Anarchitecte to arrive, he tries to imagine Richard Greaves's garbological assemblages in terms of whatever comes to mind, no, he doesn't have enough of an imagination to construct compelling visions out of Richard Greaves's installations without the aid of additional photographs of his installations, in other words (1) his imagination seems to subsist on the hope that a vague juxtaposition of data signals from disparate sources might yield an associative thread of interest, (2) it is likely the decision-management hub that has shuttered his windows into nature is also responsible for shuttering his windows into visual art, such that the only piece from all the modern art museums he has visited in the last twelve years that has stayed with him is an erased movie at the MoMA in New York (and here Antonio searches online for MoMA + movie + erased + free jazz and doesn't find what he's looking for so he searches his old journals for the name of the piece, hoping this search will yield an associative thread of interest (his journal pages during his first trip to New York in October 2010 are empty so he browses through the video catalogue of the MoMA online and eventually finds it, The Death of Tom by Glenn Ligon—after footage of his reenactment of the last scene of a silent-film adaptation of Uncle Tom's Cabin was processed, the gallery label text says, Ligon discovered that the film was blurred and the imagery had disappeared and yet the artist recognized an affinity between this spectral footage and his own earlier work—no, Antonio thinks, nothing of interest for him here except the memory of him watching Ligon's spectral footage in a dark room for an hour or two—perhaps memories in which we see ourselves from a dubious omniscient vantage are uncanny not because of their content, Antonio writes, but because of the vantage from which we see ourselves—there I am in the dark in New York watching an erased movie and that person who's me cannot see the observer behind me who's also me—)), and then Antonio wonders if perhaps it isn't just his windows into nature or visual art that had been shuttered by the inordinate amount of time he has spent pretending he isn't where he is but all his windows into the outside world, including the ones that look out into what is happening to his sister, in other words Antonio receives a call from the private investigator hired by Ron the Bail Bondsman in Baltimore to interrogate him about his sister's whereabouts and Antonio tells him no one in our family knows where she is because my sister believes our family + the Pentagon + Obama are conspiring against her, and after the call with the private investigator ends the windows into what has been happening to his sister (losing her job as a Senior Actuarial Associate, losing her house, fleeing Baltimore before a judge would deem her mentally incapable to stand trial for allegedly threatening to shoot her neighbors) shut and he goes on living inside his Richard Greaves assemblage without his sister's misfortunes, without calls from private investigators, without visual art, without nature, without descriptions of landscapes or nature anywhere in his recollections of his Jesuit school years in Bogotá, and although at first he'd thought he was against descriptions of nature in his fiction due to his affinity with the aesthetics of Doing Without, he has come to believe that all these years pretending he hasn't been running SQL queries eight hours a day inside a cubicle in the financial district of Los Angeles not only have given birth to this decision-management hub that has erased nature for him but have also atrophied this decision-management hub such that it has begun to erase everything at random, yes, so much of his life in the last twelve years has consisted of erasures that have included nature, visual art, his sister, hundreds of passages about avant-garde music that he'd tried to commingle with passages about his Jesuit school days in Bogotá, and while he waits for Richard Greaves Anarchitecte to arrive he wonders if searching for all the other passages he has erased in the last twelve years might yield an associative thread of interest, and it occurs to Antonio that as the erasures have accumulated throughout the years his imagination has had to subsist on a pool of material that's now a puny fraction of his original material, in other words perhaps all he has left is his Jesuit school in Bogotá and the music of Arvo Pärt / Olivier Messiaen he has been listening to while writing about his life at his Jesuit school in Bogotá, and yet if he were to write about nature for the Nature issue of Conjunctions perhaps he would be better off skipping any mention of decision-management hubs born out of pretending he isn't where he is or any mention of windows or erasures and focus instead on what still remains for him of nature: there was once a barren soccer field at San Luis Gonzaga High School in Bogotá where I would play soccer every day with friends I haven't seen since I moved to the United States twenty-one years ago, and my friend Rafael would kick the ball so out-of-bounds, toward the giant palm trees surrounding the soccer field, that we used to call him Monkey Shooter, and whenever we needed a quick rest we would sit on rocks like prehistoric eggs next to Don Jacinto's cafeteria and prattle about the future of Colombia, that is all that comes to mind when I think about nature, Antonio would write in his essay about nature, I am not a nostalgic but that is all that nature means to me, thank you for asking (and then a week later the bail bondsman calls his work phone again and says the ten days are up and if his private investigators can't find his sister Antonio and his mother will have to pay the $110,000 as per the bail bond contract they signed, and then Richard Greaves Anarchitecte arrives in the mail and Antonio contemplates photographs of his installations, hoping to find an associative thread of interest (no, Antonio thinks, nothing except Greaves's spiderwebs of twine, perhaps Antonio prefers these assemblages to exist for him as they have existed for him before, as vague hubs of vague associations — I make the shape of the house with the twine, Richard Greaves says, then I build — such that if a wind came and swept it all only these skeletons of twine would remain)).

F8

WHEN ESTELA WAS ANTONIO

Your sister wrote beautiful letters, Antonio's mother says, when she was nine or ten your grandfather called me from Chapel Hill and said Estela is going to be a writer, Leonora, she has written us a fantastic letter that reads like an adventure story in which Estela's stranded at the Miami airport with her mother who doesn't speak English and her baby brother who drools, because due to a mishap by the travel agency in Bogotá, Antonio's sister wrote, my Mom was told at the counter in Miami that she had to pay extra to fly back to Bogotá but she didn't have extra to fly back to Bogotá, grandpa, imagine that, my Mom only had a few dollars in her pocket and no credit cards even though you told her to apply for a credit card for emergencies, so there we were, grandpa, stranded at the Miami airport without money, without food, sharing our sad tale with a Cuban waitress so she would bring us free orange juice and crackers, and at this juncture in the recording Antonio's mother repeats the words historia jocosa, which Antonio will try not to translate as jocular story, his mother repeating that his sister's letter was a jocular adventure story as if unconvinced by her dramatization of the jocular aspects of his sister's letter, and years later your grandfather shared that letter with me, Antonio's mother says, and I asked him if I could keep it and he said no, Leonora, you've already read it, this letter was meant for us, plus whenever I'm upset or worried I read it again and laugh, didn't my sister study literature in high school, Antonio says, she was fascinated by books, Antonio's mother says, she would read all the time and write wonderful book summaries, whereas for math she would cry that she didn't want to learn math do you remember she would read the books that had been assigned to you and she would summarize them for you, no I don't remember, Antonio says, remember when you won that book contest even though you hadn't read the book, Antonio's mother says, The Metamorphosis, Antonio says, your sister was the one who summarized that book for you, Antonio's mother says, and you didn't want to win that contest but you did and you had to present it in front of the whole school so you would say to your sister help me, please, no Toñio now you have to read the book, she was such a quick reader and I would say to her Estelita what's that book about, and she would summarize it for me, but read it Mom, she would say, I don't have time please summarize it for me, I would say, and she would tell me, but after she graduated from high school she didn't read anymore, when I grow up I am going to have my own money so that no man will mistreat me, your sister would say, and so after high school she stopped reading and focused on studying finance, numbers, which she was never very good at, studying and working with numbers overextended her, Antonio, but she had this need to feel financially secure so she sacrificed what she was good at, don't you remember you used to write, I would say to her, no Mom I don't remember, don't you remember you used to write to your grandparents, no Mom I don't remember, that humorous letter like an adventure story you sent to your grandparents, no Mom, that jocular letter that I didn't find after your grandfather passed away, Antonio's mother says, although I did find many of the other letters you and your sister sent to your grandparents but not that one — dear grandparents I want to thank you for the pistol, Antonio wrote, I also want to inform my uncle Luis that if I visit this summer I am not going to break his airplanes because I build airplanes too and know how hard it is to assemble them — dear grandparents I'm in second place at school, Antonio's sister wrote, but if I get twenty over twenty in music and the boy who is in first place gets sixteen over twenty then I will be the best student—my sister stopped reading completely and never wanted to talk about books, Antonio says, because it reminded her of how much she used to enjoy it, Antonio's mother says, and look how your lives turned out, Antonio, the one who became a writer is you.

THE REVISIONIST BY HELEN SCHULMAN

Why not not do something as inevitable as being home on time for dinner, Antonio reads, not remembering having read this or any other thought from Hershleder, the protagonist of The Revisionist, which Antonio has been rereading for almost a decade, and although he doesn't ever remember too many specifics from The Revisionist, he does remember this short fiction as (1) a performance of delay, (2) too dependent on its reversal at the end, (3) paradoxical because despite knowing about (2) he always cries in the end, and of course once he rereads The Revisionist, as he's doing now, Hershleder's delay becomes less about (1)(2)(3) and more about Hershleder's desire to delay his trajectory back home, Hershleder's desire being Antonio's desire, of course, though less so over the years, yes, why not watch a movie during the day instead of going home, Hershleder thinks, why not enter the Silver Horse, as Antonio had done many years ago as he waited for an acquaintance to let him into a nightclub nearby (how ridiculous the word nightclub sounds to him now—just as ridiculous as all those years I wanted the freedom to exhaust myself at nightclubs, Antonio writes—), and so as he waited for his nightclub acquaintance, Antonio hesitated about entering the Silver Horse because he liked to believe he wasn't the type to enter the Silver Horse or any other so-called gentleman's club due to a faulty youthful logic of why pay for women to dance for me if I can just pick them up at nightclubs—completely different pleasures, Antonio writes—the fading wise man of the flesh, eh?—go away—and yet to pass the time that night almost a decade ago he did enter the Silver Horse, where he discovered a glass room like an aquarium that the manage-

ment had named the Smoking Room, and because this room
had been built by the management in the back, facing the stage,
and because this room had been sealed by the management
such that inside the music sounded muffled — ahora ya soy un
Axolotl — Antonio could watch the dancers on the stage and the
men interacting with the dancers working the floor as if he were
watching a television show with the sound off, with the added benefit that he didn't feel as guilty about staring at the dancers from
inside the aquarium, plus every now and then the dancers
would step out of the television and into the aquarium and ask
him for his name, a smoke, a dance, and so every Friday or
Thursday, soon after marrying his future former wife, who was
already four or five months pregnant with Ada, he wouldn't do
something as inevitable as being home for his future former
wife, but instead he would switch on the television at the Silver
Horse for an hour or two — a show without consequences, Antonio writes, unlike pursuing women at nightclubs — and one evening, during summer #1, while his (not yet) former wife and his
newborn were in Czechia with Babička and Děda, he switched
on the television to find the most beautiful woman he'd ever
seen in his life — call me Hari — and she stepped out of the television and into the aquarium, lit a Camel Light, and then (and
he will never forget this moment — I will never forget this moment, Antonio writes — a moment he hasn't shared with anyone because who wants to hear about a thirty-year-old South
American flummoxed by a beautiful hippie at a strip club? — the
moment when he said to himself dear god — dear god who
doesn't exist, Antonio writes — dear god, please, just this once,
inhaling and summoning all the available knowledge he'd accumulated over his thirty years of life and then) he said this,
that, everything, anything she might care about, Che Guevara,
she said, his biography by Jon Lee Anderson, he said, which

he'd happened to have been reading, recent graduate of Ever-
green State College, she said, Grateful Dead concerts with my
parents when I was a child, she said, and so they exchanged
phone numbers and a week later they drove together to Burning
Man, a party in the desert marketed as a transcendental utopia
that is just an excuse for Americans to consume psychedelic
drugs—welcome home!—what's your playa name?—Cosmic
Harenina at your service—Berthe Trépat at your service—
joven!—and perhaps years from now, when he's old and alone
and banished from his loved ones, he will no longer remember
that their safeword was elephant, or that Hari, the most beautiful
woman he'd ever encountered, would politely request that he
slap her legs, face, thighs, that he tie her to chairs, drag her by a
dog collar to a water bowl on his kitchen floor—I didn't know I
could be into this, Antonio writes—and perhaps years from now
he will no longer remember the night he'd shown up at the
Silver Horse at 1:45 a.m. and she'd told him to wait for her
outside but on the corner nearby because she wasn't allowed
to leave with customers, and so he waited for her on the corner nearby and she swung open the door of a taxi still in
motion and said quick, jump in, and so he jumped into the taxi
as if into a toboggan—wheeeee—and inside the taxi she pro-
voked him on purpose so he would slap her in the face, and he
did comply and slap her in the face—don't mind us we're role-
playing—and when they arrived at her rundown hotel near Venice Beach and she said quick I am not allowed to bring anyone
with me and there's cameras everywhere—the closet-sized room
in a sliver of hotel inserted between buildings as an afterthought
where she was living in complete squalor, Antonio writes, the
floor and bed and desk covered in vintage summer dresses, glitter, handmade leg warmers, which were banned from the Silver
Horse soon after—no hippies allowed, buddy—but what

Antonio will never forget, even when he's old and alone and banished from his loved ones, is that moment he said dear god, please, just this once—dear god, Antonio said when he saw Dora for the first time, please don't let me approach her I have a three-year-old daughter at home—dear god, Antonio said when he saw his former wife for the first time at a ski cabin in Tahoe, her face as red as a lobster because she'd snowboarded without sunblock, dear god please end her relationship with that retrograde investment banker soon—a lobster is an excellent choice—and god said goddamn it, Drool, fine, just this once—will you forget Hari's voice, too?—I used to ask Hari to leave messages on my voicemail just so I could hear her voice, Antonio writes, a voice I can't describe without thinking of preschool, mantel, nurse—Hari did volunteer at Casa Linda, a preschool in Santa Monica, Antonio writes, the same preschool my daughters would attend years later—sana sana / culito de rana—and when you are old and alone and banished from your loved ones, you will dial the deathbed number assigned to you and Hari's voice will tell you again no se que decirte pero, how do you say it, me gustas mucho?—commuters, Hershleder thinks, men who travel to and from their wives, their children, the office, men with secret lives in foreign lands, Hershleder thinks, who delay going home by having yet another round of drinks, and although Hershleder doesn't delay his trajectory back home by entering a so-called gentleman's club or attending Burning Man with a dancer from the Silver Horse—while in his heart he lusted after irresponsibility, Hershleder thinks, he was never bad enough—pues fíjate que yo sí—and here Antonio, proud of his former irresponsibility, decides not to search for the divorce papers his former wife filed five years ago, as soon as Eva was born, which document the consequences of his irresponsibility (but of course Antonio does search for them and does reread them—Antonio goes out partying several times a week, his former wife wrote, usually around 7:00 p.m. and doesn't return until three or four in the morning—I am frightened of him and frightened for the welfare of my daughters, his former wife wrote—), Hershleder does encounter someone in the subway who sells him a Thai stick, which he does smoke, and so the ghosts that lived inside him, Hershleder thinks, spiraled around in concentric circles—I ask the court to order a random full-panel alcohol and drug test, his former wife wrote—and so Hershleder decides to walk a mile and a half to Itty and the kids, a mile and a half from his home and future heart failures, Hershleder thinks, and as Antonio rereads The Revisionist, he wonders if he should start adding a date next to the passages he has underlined and will underline as a way to track what has mattered to him about Hershleder's trajectory over the years, or perhaps he should add a date next to the passages he should have underlined but didn't—there was a locker room of vile language in the homeless woman's head, Antonio doesn't underline, but her face seemed apologetic—he made a mental note to give in to Itty, Antonio underlines, she'd been begging him to agree to get a pup for the kids, 9 12-15-22-5 25-15-21, Antonio underlines, stopping to decode what Hershleder's son had once said to Hershleder at bedtime, bringing tears to Hershleder's eyes, and just as Antonio can never remember too many specifics from The Revisionist after he's done rereading it, he can't remember if in his previous readings he'd also stopped at this juncture in The Revisionist, three pages away from the end, once Hershleder has reached the front porch of his house, hesitating, thinking of his wife, Itty, the potter, hungry for connection, attention, stopping at this juncture of The Revisionist and thinking why go on, I know how it ends and I don't feel like reading three more pages of short sentences in English, and so he stops reading and goes to sleep—good night Hershleder, good night Hari—and weeks later his former wife says your daughters want a dog and he says no, we don't need a dog, what difference would a dog make in our lives, a dog won't exist for me just as the outside world doesn't exist for me, just as his sister doesn't exist for him unless he receives calls from the owner of Any Day Bail Bonding asking for his money, as Antonio does the next morning on his work phone at Prudential Investments, you and your mother signed her bail, Ron Graebel says, you are responsible for her, my sister's disappearance is a tragedy for our family, Antonio says, especially for my mother, who can't endure the thought that her daughter might be living in a homeless shelter somewhere in the United States, this shows a welcome sincerity, Ron Graebel says, it is disheartening to us to have your private investigators threatening us over the phone, Antonio says, I'm not aware of any specifics as to dealings you have had with the investigators they are financially motivated to find her, Ron Graebel says, it is unnecessarily callous to call my uncle Lucho to make accusations that my mother is hiding my sister in Colombia, Antonio says, I did hear from my office manager that you have been uncooperative with them, Ron Graebel says, I understand you have a business to run but can we avoid adding more suffering to the already unbearable suffering my mother is going through, Antonio says, the investigators deal with all sorts in our business and at times it's hard to know who is sincere and who is lying, Ron Graebel says, this is not some theoretical suffering I am talking about, Antonio says, I am sure they are as frustrated as you are, Ron Graebel says, my mother is physically ill from everything that has been transpiring with my sister, Antonio says, keep in mind they are trying to save you from paying the full bail amount, Ron Graebel says, but I will speak to them and convey your thoughts, and weeks later Antonio returns to that sentence he'd underlined in The Revisionist about giving in to Itty about getting a pup, and once again Hershleder's reaching the front porch of his house, and a young jogger is entering Hershleder's house, and Hershleder is wondering what's the meaning of this, and Hershleder's jamming his key at a lock that doesn't fit, and Hershleder's ringing the bell and waking everyone up and Hershleder and the jogger are shouting at each other, please, sweetheart, Hershleder's wife says to the jogger (to the jogger!), and she's sitting on the slate steps and explaining to him, Dr. David Hershleder, M.D., patiently and for the thousandth time, that this is no longer his home, that he has to stop coming around here, upsetting her, upsetting the children, that it's time, Dave, to take a good look at himself, when all Hershleder is capable of looking at is her, his wife, sitting with him on the stoop of his house in his neighborhood while his children cower inside.

I was an accident, Katerina said, and because both of my parents were still in graduate school, they shipped me to Seoul to live with my grandmother, what were they studying, Antonio said, physics, Katerina said, pausing because their waiter was approaching with an ice bucket for their bottle of Cava, and then or later Katerina didn't comment on the solemn Arvo Pärt concert they had heard at Disney Hall, which looks like a Marriott hotel inside, incidentally, but she did seem delighted to answer all of Antonio's questions about her upbringing even though she'd just met him via Your Sugar Arrangements, and perhaps because of the bottle of Cava or the exaggerated height of her heels, or because of her asymmetrical purple hair or her boredom with the admiring stares around her, or because neither Antonio nor Katerina had any expectations of courtship, loveship, marriage, Antonio was delighted, too—it was all so wonderful and forbidden that I wanted nothing more in this world, Bohumil Hrabal writes, and I resolved to save eight hundred and more a week selling hot frankfurters because at last I'd found a beautiful and noble aim—as carefree as Antonio had been when, in an identical so-called upscale setting but in different restaurants, he'd met with Fiona, Akira, Valerie, Charlotte, Yoko, all of them invented names attached to YSA usernames like Little Birdie, Evil Evie, Lolita in Venice, Uzi Kitten, Giggle Girl, and one of them was a student at Columbia whose thesis was about fog and chaos theory, and Melanie played for a Chinese ensemble and wanted an adventure before returning to Stanford, and Hana from UC Riverside wanted someone to take her out to a nice dinner every now and then, and Lulu had metal braces on her teeth and did research on algebraic topology and had always fantasized about being a call girl, and Silvina II, his favorite, whose body was covered in cut marks, lived with her parents in Santa Monica and wanted an occasional allowance for tattoos, and so far most of them had no qualms about sharing their earliest memories with him, which he tries to write down the morning after meeting them — how else will I remember any of them? — I remember riding inside the front basket of my mother's bicycle on our way to school, Fiona said — I remember my mother unbuckling her baby carrier from her shoulders and putting me down on a chair at the airport, Charlotte said, soon after she'd adopted me, and I became so desperate that I fell to the floor as I tried to reach her — and if his so-called sugar arrangements happen to ask him why he has joined what in public he likes to call our beloved website, he tells them the heroin + internet executive + yacht + black widow backstory, and they both laugh and Antonio toasts to not being dead, and sometimes, in his extra-small studio apartment, also known as The Other Home, which consists of one platform bed without legs and seven bookshelves with hundreds of novels in English and Spanish — have you read them all, Arturo? — no but all of them have bookmarks on the last page I read of them — he has to cover their mouths so as to not wake up his neighbors (Antonio would rather not think about that now — are you embarrassed to think about sex while at your place of employment, Drool? — yes so what? — the selectively prudish database analyst ha ha — shut up —), and if any of his so-called sugar arrangements falls asleep (after doing what Antonio would rather not think about now), as Antonio often does since he has been scheduling two new sugar arrangements per week and still has to wake up early for his database analyst job, he lets them sleep because why would he wake up a beautiful college student and ask her to leave, although if they stay past

4:00 a.m. he's barely able to sleep, sliding between apparitions of his former wife banging on his front door and the sounds of his wall heater, of his neighbors opening and closing drawers in search of teacups or spoons, of the 6:00 a.m. garbageman dragging recycling bins down the steep flight of stairs underneath his apartment, and if they happen to say what about you, Arturo, what is your earliest memory of childhood, Antonio says (in a cheerful tone that avoids hints of submerged disturbances) unfortunately I don't remember anything about my childhood, which is true, and of course none of them press him as to why he doesn't remember anything about his childhood, just as none of them press him about why he can only meet them after 9:30 p.m. during the week, not that he's going to tell them the truth if they do press him—I have to draw numbers on my daughters' backs at 8:45 p.m. before bedtime—and sometimes, on his way to meet his so-called sugar arrangements, the driver of the car he has ordered at 9:15 p.m. mistakenly parks in front of the apartment where his daughters have just fallen asleep, three doors down from him, and he has to call the driver and say can you please back up I will explain in a second—ugh—and because he always meets them after 9:30 p.m. he doesn't have to worry about receiving calls or messages from Ron the Bail Bondsman demanding his money or from his sister's attorney in Baltimore informing Antonio that his sister has faxed a medical form from an ambulatory community health center in Milwaukee—dear Thomas, his sister wrote, I have followed the court requirement to see a doctor but I can't go back to Maryland due to lack of appropriate shelter and employment—and Lina from Mills College has been dating older men since high school but joined YSA for a week so she could buy her best friend a bicycle, and Silvina III from UCLA had never been to a nice restaurant before and she was so surprised she was enjoying herself that she said you're doing such a good job seducing me, Arturo—who will ever want to hear about how much I loved her long bowed legs, Antonio writes, which I will never see again?—when my mother was mad she would use metaphors that made no sense, Anna said, the house is messy like a calendar, she would say—my mother was a set designer for movies, a freshman at the Rhode Island School of Design said, and she would take me with her to the prop stores, did you have a favorite movie set, Antonio said, Elektra in New York because its set had a strange shop that required my mother and I to shop for doll heads though the movie was never finished—high school teachers should be required to draw a diagram of life on the board and explain that one day everyone will age horribly, Antonio said to Katerina, and that in the finite number of years before they become ambulatory carcasses, they should enjoy their bodies without worrying about ridiculous concepts like monogamy and marriage, which were probably invented by ancient carcasses trying to constrain their spirited young wives, and don't listen to anyone who tells you an excess of sex will result in an excess of punishment because no punishment will come for enjoying yourself if you are careful about concealing your excesses—I like learning, sex, and spending money, Gloria said—and when years later my mother was finally done with her graduate program in physics she came to visit me in Seoul, Katerina said, and I remember thinking who is this pretty lady, pausing because their waiter was approaching with their tray of oysters, although when my mother told me not to eat candy before dinner I rushed to the kitchen and said grandma, Katerina said, grandma, you need to beat up that woman.

A LEXICON OF TERROR & OTHER STORIES BY
SNÆBORG OCAMPO

Borges concealed his fondness for mirrors by affirming the opposite, the narrator of Mirrors Aren't Terrifying says, a narrator
called Jules Jakobsdóttir who's lecturing her bathroom mirror
about how she isn't amused by her reflection across multiple dimensions because (a) multiple dimensions are a cliché and (b)
they are probably a sign she needs medication, which is strange
because she's already on medication ha ha, and in some dimensions a benevolent professor version of herself lectures the bathroom mirror version of herself about the ontology of clichés—if
you no longer speak your native language on a daily basis, Professor Jakobsdóttir says, nostalgia will exalt the clichés of your
native language—and in other dimensions a dentist version of
herself offers the bathroom mirror version of herself LSD instead of Novocain for reasons that will only become apparent to
readers of The God of the Labyrinth, and in this dimension, the
one where Antonio is rereading Mirrors Aren't Terrifying, the first
story in A Lexicon of Terror & Other Stories by Silvina, he can't
recall if he'd told Silvina that the concept of a reflection across
multiple dimensions reminded him of something Peter Ström, a
New Age therapist, had told him during one of the two constellation therapies Antonio underwent with him, back when Antonio and his former wife were still trying to separate without
rupturing their daughters' lives—but before I tell you what Peter
Ström told me, Antonio writes, I would like to explain that, in
constellation therapy, facilitators like Peter Ström operate under
the assumption that present difficulties are influenced by trau-
mas suffered in previous generations of the family, even if those

affected now are unaware of the original events in the past, and these systemic entanglements, as Hellinger calls them, or invisible loyalties, as Iván Böszörményi-Nagy calls them, or quantum quackery, as cynics like me call them, or los tentáculos invisibles, as my mother, a facilitator like Peter Ström, probably doesn't call them, are said to occur when unresolved trauma has afflicted a family through an event such as murder, suicide, incest, death of a mother in childbirth, war, emigration, abuse, in other words an event so traumatic that it causes a rift in the family system—there is a deep need for justice and retribution within family systems, Hellinger says—in other words even if you luck out and your father isn't as horrifying as mine, Antonio writes, you're still probably doomed by a suicidal uncle you and your parents didn't even know—and now that I've explained constellation therapy, Antonio writes, I would like to explain the mechanics of the therapy itself—although here Antonio stops writing and tries to remember the steep stairs to Peter Ström's subterranean home in Hollywood Hills, which at the time didn't bring to mind his psychotherapy sessions with Dr. Adler in a subterranean office in Santa Monica almost ten years prior to his first constellation therapy—my objective is to peel myself like an artichoke and become who I am in a year, he'd said to Dr. Adler during his first session with her, and five years later they would sometimes joke about what he'd said to her in that first session—I am exhausted by this ceaseless examining of myself, he'd said to Dr. Adler during his final session with her, I can't keep battling these inherited undercurrents—and after descending toward an audience of ten or twelve people in Peter Ström's pleasant living room in Hollywood Hills, Antonio's former wife says to Peter Ström my husband and I want to work on our relationship, so Peter Ström draws family charts on a chalkboard for both him and his former wife and asks her to pick representatives from the audience so that one of these representatives will become her father, one of them will become her grandmother (he doesn't remember what any of these representatives looked like, except Peter Ström, who looked like J. M. Coetzee, at ease in his humorlessness), and these representatives aren't told what his former wife's parents were like, but they are told by Peter Ström to behave whichever way they feel in the moment, in other words you're vessels of complex energetic forces, Peter Ström says, and because Antonio's former wife was raised by her grandmother in Czechia, a grandmother who protected his former wife from her older, abusive sister, a grandmother he can easily imagine because his former wife has told him about her and there's a picture on the fridge of this grandmother holding his former wife when she was a baby, and since this grandmother died when his former wife was thirteen, when the representative for her grandmother says to his former wife I want to hold on to you forever, please don't let me go, his former wife cries inconsolably, and Peter Ström says you can't start your own family if you don't let your grandmother go, do let her go, tell her you love her and say goodbye, but his former wife refuses, she cries inconsolably and refuses, and then he's in a different constellation therapy session months later and the representative for his mother says I am scared of you, or perhaps he is the one saying to the representative for his mother I think you are scared of me, and then Antonio and the representative for his mother jostle each other because Peter Ström has asked Antonio to hold hands with his mother but instead of holding hands they're clasping their hands as if trying to push each other off a ring, and at some point, before or after the jostling with his mother, Peter Ström picks a sturdy man from the audience and tells him to stand behind Antonio and place his arms on Antonio's shoulders, a sturdy man who isn't a representative of any family member of yours, Peter Ström says, but a representative of all men across multiple generations, which is what Silvina's concept of a reflection across multiple dimensions brought to mind as he read Mirrors Aren't Terrifying for the first time, soon after Silvina & Antonio started sneaking into each other's life during summer #7.

—

Ulrica Thrale (the protagonist of Ramifications of Scholarships) boosts her college application by playacting on the cello, the harpsichord, the viola—show me the version where I play the triangle, Ulrica Thrale says—jokes do pass the time, Ulrica Thrale's best friend says—by performing a panoply of extracurricular activities that might impress the college admissions officials, but unfortunately every extracurricular activity ramifies into other extracurricular activities—the cello ramified into learning Italian → volunteering at The Cinematheque → handmaking kaleidoscopes, Ulrica Thrale says—and because her parents aren't around to advise her against submitting her complete ramifications, she submits a college application the size of an encyclopedia, which clearly (according to the admissions letter that Ulrica Thrale never receives) is a sign of the applicant's brilliance, and although Silvina didn't submit a college application the size of an encyclopedia, she did try to impress the admissions officials with a panoply of extracurricular activities to be admitted to Princeton, which is also what Antonio had done to be admitted to Yale, after he graduated from high school in Bogotá and arrived in Chapel Hill, North Carolina, starting a newspaper at his community college and volunteering at Big Brothers Big Sisters so he could be considered as a transfer student to Yale or Harvard or Stanford—I attended a Jesuit high school in Bogotá, Antonio writes, and although my grades were almost perfect, I was often suspended from

school for misconduct—please don't expel Antonio this time
he did have an altercation with his father, Father Ignacio—such
that when the time came for me to apply to Yale and Harvard
and Stanford I had to write a long letter to the principal of San
Luis Gonzaga begging him to please answer no to the question
in the college application asking if this student ever had any
behavioral problems at school—and yet according to Antonio
he'd wanted to be admitted to Yale or Harvard or Stanford not
because he wanted to change his miserable life, as Ulrica Thrale
was trying to do—when I arrived at Princeton I thought at last I
have ceased to be what I have been, Silvina said—all of your priors will be expunged and none of your priors will be expunged
do you understand, Ulrica Thrale's math teacher says—but because he needed to prepare himself for the great task of returning to Colombia and running for office so he could save the
poor and so on, and yes, he did possess this impulse to return to
Colombia to run for office, but one of the many aspects of Ramifications of Scholarships that disrupted his attempts at writing
fiction was Silvina's openness in writing about her own shame
about having less money than others, an openness Antonio
didn't possess back then because there was no way he was going to acknowledge to anyone, even to himself, that part of the
reason he'd never returned to Colombia to run for office had to
do with finally having a job in Los Angeles that allowed him to
have enough money to spend on expensive clothes—my mother
glued acrylic nails inside our garage, Antonio writes, which she
had converted into a nail salon where she also sold difficult to
find imports like Toblerones, and since we didn't have a car I
always had to beg my classmates for a ride, such that I had to
drop out of tennis lessons after school when I was in elementary
school because no one could give me a ride back home—your

son has tremendous potential in tennis please find a way for him to continue lessons, Doña Leonora — and perhaps because during summer #7 Silvina was living in such precarious conditions (she had just graduated with a masters in neuroscience, her boyfriend had broken up with her so she had to move out of his apartment to a temporary sublet above Gratitude Cafe, didn't have a job yet and didn't have the kind of parents who could provide financial assistance — dear financial aid office at Yale I misled you when I wrote down that my mother's annual income was $700, Antonio writes, I was too embarrassed to ask my mother how much she accumulated per year from her acrylic nails garage business — dear financial aid office at Yale the summer before flying to you I sold Hawaiian shirts at the mall so I could afford the plane ticket from Chapel Hill to New Haven, Antonio writes — dear financial aid office at Yale I will always love you —), Antonio had felt a kinship with Silvina, although he didn't think about her in terms of kinship back then, when he would drive her home whenever they ran into each other at the literature in translation series at Skylight Books and she would answer his questions awkwardly and he would try not to flirt with her because he was sure she was waiting for him to flirt with her just so that she could say to her friends see, these Latin American men are all alike, sure she was worried he was going to reach across and grab her leg any minute now as he drove her to her sublet above Gratitude Cafe, and yet one night, out of despair or boredom or because here was this beautiful science fiction writer on his passenger seat, Antonio said to her I don't feel like going home yet would you like to stop for a drink somewhere, and Silvina said sure, and Antonio said great (and not much else so as to not risk blurting out anything that could change her mind), driving to Tabula Rasa on Hollywood Boulevard, where their knees almost touched as they half swiveled on the barstools not out of coquetry but because they were both anxiously fishing for statements in each other's monologues that could feed their own monologues so as to cast a loop of compatibilities, in other words they were trying to create the illusion of fluidity because according to the mating culture of the United States fluidity amounted to chemistry, and this so-called chemistry was supposed to be a good sign and not just one accretion of traumas called Antonio at birth sniffing another accretion of traumas called Silvina at birth and saying, like the song in that movie where Philip Seymour Hoffman listens to an ersatz god on an earpiece before he dies alone, I know you, you're the one I've waited for — my father lives in a homeless shelter, Antonio — soon my sister will live in a homeless shelter too, Silvina — and after they finished their drinks at Tabula Rasa they danced to dancehall in a corner of the bar and he asked her if it was okay if he flirted with her and she said yes, and so he kissed her, and so they exited the bar and they entered her temporary bedroom above Gratitude Cafe, where he discovered Silvina's predilections weren't too dissimilar from Hari's — elephant? — no, Antonio writes, Silvina picked László Krasznahorkai as her safeword to amuse me — and where, the next morning, he awoke to discover he was still there — dinosaur jokes straight to the left, sir, Augusto Monterroso says — and although he doesn't remember everything they said to each other the next morning, he likes to believe he will always remember her box set of the complete works of Silvina Ocampo, which he encountered in her temporary kitchen and which he carried to her temporary bedroom, where he said are you trying to change your name to Silvina so you can say you wrote these, and Silvina said my Venezuelan father wanted to call me Silvina but my Icelandic mother hated my father so much that she picked a name he couldn't pronounce, and because Silvina frowned at Antonio every time he called her Silvina, twisting her mouth in disapproval, he continued to call her Silvina, exaggerating his fake Italian accent so that it sounded like Silvína.

—

Parallel Longings, the most experimental of Silvina's stories, is written in the form of a Q&A with the chatbot of a detective agency called Parallel Longings, which clients hire to investigate what happens in their parallel lives — our detectives have special access to subspace corridors, the chatbot replies to the question how do your detectives travel between parallel lives — and as Antonio rereads Parallel Longings, imagining its subspace corridors as those apocryphal tunnels connecting monasteries to convents in the Dark Ages or the Renaissance or whenever, he tries not to populate these subspace corridors with his sister, with images of his sister pacing back and forth along the subspace corridor linking her to him and deciding to fly from Baltimore to Los Angeles to spend one day with him, months before her mind was overlaid with too many errors of comprehension — does the white noise of airplanes soothe you as much as it soothes me? — who is this? — topo number two — my answer is your answer, Toñito — on long airplane rides to Czechia the white noise of the plane would blank my ability to read and all I could manage to do was watch saccharine movies featuring charming reversals, Silvina — and what I wanted to tell you, Antonio writes, no, I don't want to tell you anything — plus you already know that, before the onset of the misfortunes that await all of you, Antonio thinks, you won't become something other than what you are, in other words if your sister spends six hours each way inside a plane to see you for a day no red alert will force you to notice her desperation, no red alert will alter the intractable passageways that constitute your so-called stable family life in Los Angeles to warn you that no one boards a plane from Baltimore to Los Angeles to see anyone for a day unless that someone is desperate to reconstitute the passageways that might reestablish who she has been before an accretion of misfortunes began to disrupt her perceptions — let's play topos, Toñito — how do you play topos? — easy just repeat after me topo / topo / topo — desperate to untrace the passageways already overtaken by conspirative voices incognizant of the spatiotemporal regulations in the USA — my little brother thinks he's better than me because he spent two years at Yale what a sham — no red alert will warn you and your former wife that if your sister spends six hours each way inside a plane to visit you for a day you probably shouldn't reprimand your sister for eating all the baby carrots in the fridge — that is so rude, Estela — just as no red alert warned Antonio that, as summer #7 was coming to an end, as his daughters and former wife were boarding a plane from Czechia to Los Angeles, he was beginning to relegate Silvina to where the rest of his former companions were already fading and not fading from him, even though he didn't want to relegate Silvina anywhere — but before I tell you about The End of Silvina I want to tell you about Thomas Bernhard, Antonio writes, about that one afternoon inside a food court sushi place in the financial district of Los Angeles where Silvina, knowing I was organizing a marathon reading of Correction by Thomas Bernhard, one sentence per person, one shot of Cava per appearance of the word Cone, surprised me by gifting me a hardcover first edition of Correction by Thomas Bernhard — she didn't have enough money for food why would she spend $35 on me? — don't be a moron, Toñio — the hardcover first edition of Correction by Thomas Bernhard with two statues on the cover that reminded him of the human figures on Easter Island, the best gift anyone had ever given him, Antonio realized as she handed him the beautiful hardcover first edition of Correction by Thomas Bernhard, displacing in seconds all the wrongheaded gifts he'd received from former girlfriends throughout the years like thin belts, boxer shorts, franchise coffee, a pillow shaped like a pair of breasts, a snowboard, and either because Correction by Thomas Bernhard was the best gift anyone had ever given him or because he already knew that Silvina would be gone from him soon after the end of summer #7, even if he didn't want to acknowledge it to himself just yet — I have come to define happiness collectively, Antonio writes, and it's ridiculous, given that most adult relationships end anyway, Antonio reassures himself, to pursue a relationship with another adult at the expense of my daughters, who are so little still — his face, trying to suppress his impulse to cry, adopted a pained look that he tried to soften by repeating thank you so much, Silvina, thank you so much — find me Silvina's hands at that precise moment please — anything you say, boss — and, a week later, at the marathon reading of Correction by Thomas Bernhard, he bunched next to Silvina at a booth in Gratitude Cafe and pretended he wasn't spending every other evening with her (why did he encourage her to keep their relationship secret? so as to not upset Silvina's friends whose advances she'd turned down in college? so that there would be less explaining to do once it was over?), and, many months later, after the relegation had been completed and Silvina's apparitions had shifted from being painful reminders of what could have been to being forms of consolation for him — where are you taking me now, Antonio? — everywhere I go you go, Silvina — he boarded a plane to Baltimore to check on his sister, who, as she became less suspicious about the purpose of his unannounced visit, ranted at him with the same fervent repetitions, the same manic delivery of Thomas

Bernhard—I don't understand why Bernhard's always so pissed, Silvina—read his autobiography?—an autobiography that chronicles Bernhard's terrible upbringing and repeatedly acknowledges how this terrible upbringing has irreversibly marked him—by means of the cruel words my mother shouted at me she achieved peace and quiet, Thomas Bernhard says, but every time they plunged me into the most terrible pit of suffering, from which I have never escaped as long as I have lived—and as Antonio rereads Thomas Bernhard's autobiography he finds in the back of it some notes he'd written years ago about a coworker of his who reminded Antonio of Doc Brown in Back to the Future, a jovial man in his seventies who'd lent him a VHS tape on Borges and had told Antonio about growing up with his eccentric parents, both of them railroad workers, Doc Brown said, and sometimes my father would appear before my mother in one of his military costumes and recite poetry to her, and my mother, not to be outdone, would unearth her toga from the closet and refute my father by reciting from her side of the poetry stack, I knew a woman, Doc Brown recited, lovely in her bones, and last year, Doc Brown said, after I awoke from a coma, the heart surgeon asked me if I understood where I was, what had happened to me, and I wanted to tell him I was fine but didn't know how, couldn't articulate a simple statement to confirm I understood him so I panicked and began to declaim from Julius Caesar, friends, I said, Romans, countrymen, lend me your ears, I come to bury Caesar, not to praise him, and so the heart surgeon called his nurses, Doc Brown said, alarmed that perhaps I'd become deranged because I was talking nonsense and crying as I remembered my parents reciting poetry to each other in our living room, my parents, both dead, whom I miss every day—I wish I had parents I could miss, Silvina—my father's medication has shriveled the tentacles that tie him to his outer galaxies, Silvina said, but he has gained so much weight that he looks as if three versions of him have been crammed into one—and perhaps this image of Doc Brown's parents reciting poetry to each other has become an essential element in Antonio's narrative of how adult relationships should unfold, Antonio thinks, or at least the kind of adult relationships he would have liked to have for himself, and yes, during summer #7 Antonio did ask Silvina to read to him, although he doesn't remember what exactly he'd asked Silvina to read to him (later he will find in his phone's iTalk app (1) a 6:17 recording of Silvina reading from War & War by László Krasznahorkai, (2) a 1:46:43 recording of his mother telling him about her childhood, soon after losing track of his sister for the first time, (3) a 37:59 recording of his sister ranting at him, which he'd secretly recorded in Baltimore in case he needed to present evidence she was not well in order to commit her to a mental institute), and yet he does remember the story Dora read to him during summer #3 on the BART train on their way to see a Chekhov play in Orinda during their weekend trip to San Francisco, a story called Gooseberries by Anton Chekhov, a bafflingly slow story centered around a stern monologue warning you about the perils of happiness—there ought to be behind the door of every happy, contented man, Chekhov says, someone standing with a hammer continually reminding him with a tap that there are unhappy people, that however happy he may be, life will show him her laws sooner or later, trouble will come for him, disease, poverty, losses, and no one will see or hear, just as now he neither sees nor hears others—an inadequate story for the occasion because Antonio & Dora were still young and light in each other's presence and they were on the BART train on their way to see a play in an outdoor theater and they were carrying a picnic basket with sparkling wine, prosciutto, baguette—but there is no man with a hammer, Chekhov says — a quiet story they brushed off, Antonio thinks, just as they brushed off the homeless man who boarded the BART train and handed out miniature sign language instructions with a plea to please help him, a man that offended Antonio because Antonio was sure the man was pretending to be a mute, and neither Antonio nor Dora nor anyone else on the train handed the man who was pretending to be a mute any change, and so the man sat there, defeated, waiting for the next train stop so he could escape his embarrassing predicament, and a UC Berkeley student who looked as if she'd just come back from a Peace Corps assignment began to speak to him in sign language, and he replied to her in sign language, and she replied to him in sign language, and he replied to her in sign language, and Dora & Antonio could hear the man who wasn't pretending to be a mute emitting guttural sounds as he spoke to her in sign language desperately, and as Antonio rereads Gooseberries by Anton Chekhov, he no longer finds the story bafflingly slow, or he does but finds the slowness reassuring, likely because he no longer feels like a carefree young man with a picnic basket, yes, (1) he has so many white hairs now that Ada has given up on plucking them, (2) after his evening soccer games his shins are so banged up that he has to submerge his legs in Epsom salt baths to feign recovery, (3) let us avoid an inventory of ailments, please, recalling instead, as he rereads Gooseberries by Anton Chekhov, that on the same BART train ride but in the other direction during an offsite in Concord for his database analyst job, months before his sister began to misperceive the inconcrete as concrete, months after he had relegated Dora to where the rest of his former companions were already fading and not fading from him, he'd listened to Mary Gaitskill reading Symbols and Signs by Nabokov on his oversized circumaural Sennheiser headphones and had thought about Dora and Chekhov and their picnic basket—so wonderful to see us again on this train, Dora—you have quite an imagination, Antonio—no, he won't relisten to Symbols and Signs by Nabokov because he knows this time Dora and Chekhov will be the background and his sister will be the foreground, but of course he does relisten to Symbols and Signs by Nabokov, in which an old Russian couple visit their son at his sanatorium on his birthday, but unfortunately they can't see him, the nurse informs them, he has tried to take his life and seeing you might disturb him—the boy, aged six, Mary Gaitskill reads, that was when he drew wonderful birds with human hands and feet—yes, Antonio thinks, no one is near his cubicle at Prudential Investments so he can listen to Symbols and Signs by Nabokov without needing to suppress tears as the old defeated Russian father says, lying to himself, that they will get their boy out of the sanatorium the next day—all this, and much more, the mother had accepted, Mary Gaitskill reads, for, after all, living does mean accepting the loss of one joy after another, not even joys in her case, mere possibilities of improvement—she thought of the recurrent waves of pain that for some reason or other she and her husband had had to endure, Mary Gaitskill reads, of the invisible giants hurting her boy in some unimaginable fashion, of the incalculable amount of tenderness contained in the world, of the fate of this tenderness, which is either crushed or wasted, or transformed into madness.

—

Jules Jakobsdóttir's daughter reads Mirrors Aren't Terrifying and concludes she can improve her mother's story with speech-to-text software, so she (i) records herself reading her mother's story, (ii) runs the speech-to-text software, (i.ii) records herself reading the speech-to-text version of her mother's story, (ii.ii) runs the speech-to-text software, (i.iii) records herself reading the speech-to-text version of the speech-to-text version of her mother's story, repeating herself until her process transforms her mother's story into Garbled Mother Generator, a story by Jules Jakobsdóttir's daughter (who also happens to be called Jules Jakobsdóttir), and just as the casual reader is about to conclude that Garbled Mother Generator by Silvina Snæborg Ocampo is a straightforward process story about teenagers and their damn electronic devices, Jules Jakobsdóttir begins to receive transmissions from the Garbled Mother Generator, which instructs her to visit her mother at her homeless shelter—apparently my sister has driven from Baltimore to Milwaukee because she'd heard the homeless shelters there were better for women, Silvina—your sister's storage, Antonio's mother said over the phone, we have to find the name of your sister's storage company in Baltimore—but by the time his mother discovered the name of the storage company in Baltimore where his sister deposited her belongings after she lost her house, all of his sister's belongings had already been auctioned off—now folks today we're going to auction off Missus Pimber's things, Israbestis Tott says, I think you all knew Missus Pimber and you know she had some pretty nice things—why worry about her things Mom don't we have enough to worry about already?—not her things Antonio her personal things that can't be replaced, Antonio's mother said—which Antonio does not want to imagine—the last time your sister came to visit me she removed all your childhood pictures from my albums to scan them and she never returned them to me, Antonio.

—

If someone would have shared with Antonio the amusing anecdote of a woman who, having had enough, drives to Washington, D.C., enters the Pentagon, asks the receptionist if she could please speak to a supervisor because her life has become unbearable due to the satellites orbiting her, please stop spying on me, Antonio would have chuckled, or perhaps Antonio would have chuckled later, once the amusing anecdote reaches the part where the receptionist at the Pentagon calls the woman's mother, and the woman's mother has to explain her daughter's unfortunate circumstances and assure her she's harmless, don't worry, the receptionist says, thousands like her arrive here every year, I'll tell her to go on home, except of course Antonio didn't chuckle when his mother called him and told him she'd received a call from the receptionist at the Pentagon — how did she manage to drive from Baltimore to Washington in her condition, Antonio? — just as Antonio doesn't chuckle now when he sees homeless people talking to themselves in downtown Los Angeles, homeless people screaming at the air or the Pentagon, for weeks Antonio could hear the screams of a homeless woman from his sixth-floor cubicle on South Flower Street, all those years prior to his sister's illness he didn't chuckle when he walked past homeless people talking to themselves because he just didn't see them, homeless people not existing for him like those thousands of inconvenient memories of childhood his mind has managed to wipe from him, hundreds of insensate people on the streets who, some would argue, would stop malfunctioning if they simply swallowed their medication — I tell you it's selfish not to take the pills because I know, Graham Caldwell says, because I take them too you understand, Dad? — except what if your acute powers of discernibility betray you without you noticing so you're suspicious of anyone who tries to convince you that you need medication, Antonio thinks, believing instead that your family is conspiring against you by asking you to please see a doctor who could prescribe the right medication for you, listen, you can't force someone into a mental institution, you can't force someone, once she's in a mental institution, to talk to you over the phone, moreover, once she's in a mental institution, she can prohibit anyone in the mental institution to talk to you or even acknowledge to you that she is there, in other words if you're suddenly afflicted by a perceptual disorder there is no way to unwind your disorder unless you agree to take your medication, in other words if you suddenly believe the inconcrete is concrete you could lose your job, as my sister did, you could threaten to shoot your neighbors and end up in jail, as my sister did, you could lose your house, as my sister did, you could decide to run away to Milwaukee after the judge finds you incompetent to stand trial, as my sister did, and yet in Baltimore there is one way to institutionalize someone without their consent: if someone fills out a form attesting that the person in question is a danger to herself, as Antonio and his mother did, the police can capture the person in question, as the Baltimore police did, and the person in question can then be institutionalized for no more than two weeks, but if during those two weeks the person in question refuses to take any medication, as Antonio's sister did, if, moreover, during those two weeks the mental institution refuses to communicate with you so you can explain the particulars of her unfortunate situation, as the New Horizons Hospital did, then after two weeks she is free to go, as Antonio's sister had been, refusing to talk to Antonio and his mother ever again because see, my mother and my brother were conspiring against me (and here Antonio tries not to think about the message he sent to the private investigator this morning informing him that his sister's probably at some homeless shelter in Milwaukee), in other words if you suddenly controvert what others agree isn't there there's no rapid process of retroversion unless you agree to swallow your medication.

—

All this, of course, Silvina reads, indeed his whole history, originated in the distant past, said Korin, and here Antonio rewinds
the recording of Silvina reading from War & War by László
Krasznahorkai, trying to remember where he'd recorded her, all
this, of course, Silvina reads, indeed his whole history, originated
in the distant past, said Korin, no, Antonio thinks, he can't remember where he'd recorded her so he rewinds the recording to
the beginning again, listening to Silvina's voice again and thinking of Krapp's Last Tape, which he'd seen once by himself when
he was still twenty-five or twenty-two and once years later with
Dora—we lay there without moving, Krapp hears himself say,
but under us all moved, and moved us, gently, up and down, and
from side to side [pause]—rewinding to the same part of the recording where Krapp talks about a woman lying stretched on the
floorboards with her hands under her head, her eyes closed, the
whole world moving under them, all this, of course, Silvina reads,
indeed his whole history, originated in the distant past, said Korin, yes, Antonio thinks, he'd seen Krapp's Last Tape twice: the
first time he'd been twenty-five or twenty-two, his sister still a
Senior Actuarial Associate in Baltimore, Dora and his former
wife and Silvina still many years in the future, and because he
was still trying to understand whether he could become a writer
he was reading everything and attending so many performances
for the first time, Waiting for Godot, for instance, Krapp's Last
Tape, both of them on the same weekend by the same theater
troupe, and what he remembers of that first performance by the
Gate Theatre from Dublin, almost fifteen years ago, aside from the
audience laughing during the banana jokes, is the feeling that
this rewinding business was as amazing a literary device as
the letter writing in Herzog by Saul Bellow, and what he remembers of that second performance by the Cutting Ball Theater,

eight or nine years later, is Dora reading his copy of Krapp's Last Tape while smoking outside the theater before the performance, and Dora's impassive presence in the audience next to him, and old Krapp so alone on the stage, passing the time before he dies by listening to tapes of himself as a young man talking about a woman whom he wishes to remember, again and again, we lay there without moving, Antonio can recite from memory, but under us all moved, which is how it had once been with Dora, with his former wife, with Silvina, although he can remember so few specifics about his time with Silvina, Silvina reading a 1,178-word sentence from War & War by László Krasznahorkai and laughing when she reached word 439 because the sentence was still going, pausing at word 839 to ask if he wanted her to keep going, of course I do, Antonio says, keep going, going on, call that going, call that on, listening to the recording of Silvina reading a sentence from War & War by László Krasznahorkai and hearing in the background the white noise of cars speeding by, which meant he'd recorded her on her temporary bed, in her second sublet apartment, near the off-ramp highway traffic, the windows in her room open because it was summer #7 still, Silvina outstretched on her bed in her cutoff jean shorts and a Motörhead T-shirt that was falling apart, her feet on my hands, Silvina & Antonio floating above the earth like Hari & Kris in Solaris, but unfortunately this is all that he can scrape out of this 6:17 recording of Silvina so he checks again to see if there's any more recordings of Silvina in his iTalk app, yes, yes there is, a fifty-five-second unlabeled recording of him testing where to place the phone in his car because he was interviewing László Krasznahorkai that week while driving him around Los Angeles: this should work, he says, [turns down music from Messiaen's Saint Francis of Assisi], can you talk a little bit while the car is running, hmmk so I, hmmk, she says, [in a Muppet voice], this is not really helpful, hmmk, he says, [in a Muppet voice, both laugh], let's try again let me ask you a question when was the last time you were really fucked, he says, [he laughs], all right, she says, [in a tone of resignation], just kidding what's your favorite book, he says, that's a nice question, she says, I think you might have been there for it heeey, [both laugh], so I am seeing that girl I think on Sunday, she says, what are you talking about Sunday is my day, he says, you are just going to have to, you're going to take a few hours off, she says, I am not sharing you with some girl who doesn't want to hang out with us, he says, [she laughs], you just said you couldn't blame her before you went on your death-wish spiral, and that's it, Antonio thinks, fifty-five more seconds of Silvina on top of the 6:17 of her reading War & War by László Krasznahorkai—perhaps my best years are gone, Krapp hears himself say, when there was a chance of happiness, but I wouldn't want them back, not with the fire in me now—Krapp should have recorded her instead of himself talking about her, Silvina—you think Krapp could withstand hearing her voice directly, Antonio?—all this, of course, Silvina reads, indeed his whole history [final time], originated in the distant past, said Korin, as far back as the time he first announced the fact that though an utterly mad world had made a madman of him, pure and simple, it didn't mean that that is entirely what he was, for while it would have been stupid to deny that sooner or later, nat-urally enough, that was how he'd finish up, or rather, sooner or later, reach a state resembling madness, it was obvious that whatever might in fact happen, madness was not a particularly unfortunate condition that one should fear as being oppressive or threatening, a condition one should be frightened of, no, not in the least, or at least he personally was not scared of it, not for a moment, for it was simply a matter of fact, as he later explained, that one day the straw actually did break the camel's back.

—

Ulrica Thrale's granddaughter (the protagonist of A Lexicon of Terror who's of course also called Ulrica Thrale) arrives at her father's sanatorium to inform him she's a management consultant now so she will be going away to Kansas City, and the next day she arrives to inform him she's an investment banker now so she will be going away to Salt Lake City—we plant cauliflowers and groundhogs in the garden here, one of the nurses says—and the next day and the next she continues to arrive at her father's sanatorium with a brand-new profession and her father always says permutations, connectives, infinitary annotations, scalars, and what Ulrica's father says to Ulrica next made Antonio cry the first time he read A Lexicon of Terror—good one, Snivel—back at the beginning of summer #7, when he'd asked Silvina to please share with him a copy of A Lexicon of Terror & Other Stories, no I don't even have a copy a Gloom Hulk who isn't me wrote those stories, she'd said, hmmk, he'd said, in that case we're going to Skylight Books to purchase a copy of A Lexicon of Terror & Other Stories, installing himself afterward at Gratitude Cafe to read Silvina's stories and Silvina saying I'm not sitting here while you compose eldritch thoughts about those stories I wrote in high school so she escapes upstairs, and although Antonio doesn't believe in so-called epiphanies he does like to believe that, as he was reading Silvina's stories for the first time, imagining Silvina's footsteps above him, he produced an actual epiphany for himself: if Silvina can write about her miserable childhood—her father covering all the mirrors in the house when he still lived with Silvina and her mother, her father recording his jumbled pronouncements that he would then send to the local radio station—so can I, and so Antonio rewrote large swaths of his first novel set in Bogotá, sharing with Silvina some of the worst episodes of his childhood in Bogotá in frantic monologues over dinner that he then assigned to his characters the next morning, and as he remembers those frantic monologues over dinner he thinks of that time during summer #7 when Silvina's sublease above Gratitude Cafe expired and she didn't know what to do with her ragged mattress, why don't you leave it on the sidewalk, Antonio said, I'm not sure I can do that, Silvina said, of course you can everyone else does, Antonio said, so he helped her haul her ragged mattress to the sidewalk in front of Gratitude Cafe, and Silvina became quiet, looked nervous, as if someone was eyeing her as the two of us carried her ragged mattress downstairs, what's the matter, Antonio said, I feel extremely uneasy about breaking any laws, she said, I think I'm afraid I'll make one mistake and be deported or end up in a homeless shelter — I don't think my mother will ever recover from knowing my sister ended up in a homeless shelter, Silvina — what about you how do you go on, Antonio? — it takes tremendous energy to keep functioning while carrying the memory of terror, Dr. Van Der Kolk says — and at Ulrica's father's sanatorium he says to her transmissions, emissions, subspace corridors, sensors, difficult job, I will write to your boss, Ulrica's father says, I will come with you.

WHEN ANTONIO WAS TOÑIO

You would spend hours playing soccer with your sister, Antonio's mother says, or you would combine your toys so that your helicopters would fly over her dollhouse and her Barbies would sunbathe inside your Star Wars station, and you would do earthquake, remember?, no, Antonio says, I don't remember, when you were done playing with Barbies, Antonio's mother says, because your sister would dress them, pick hats and purses for them, parade them, allow them to ride in your helicopters, the two of you would spend hours playing with your toys, and all of a sudden, perhaps because you were tired, you would do earthquake and the dollhouse would fly out in pieces and your sister would run out and say Mom my brother did earthquake on my house, so that would be the end of your games for the day, but other than that the two of you got along very well, playing soccer or hide-and-seek in our patio since we couldn't leave that house in Mirandela because your father would lock it before going to work, eventually he handed me a key after I protested so much, although I couldn't leave the house just the same because he would call every fifteen minutes, and if I didn't answer the phone, he would imagine I wasn't home and that would turn into a terrible altercation, so you would arrive home from school and we would spend our time playing together, and because you wanted to play soccer we spent a lot of time in the patio, and you would climb on the fence, standing on the ledge of the cement wall below and attaching yourself to the wire mesh above, and from up there you would chat with Don Jorge, the elderly man next door who would always say to me Leonora, if anything happens, because he would hear your father screaming and threatening us, if he lays a finger on you or something happens, you shout for us and I'll come out immediately, Don Jorge would say, and I have a gun, and one day he said to your father we're here, next door to you, and we've been listening to your screaming, you know I am armed and all I have to do is jump over the fence and bring my sons with me, who were huge, by the way, you want to act macho with your wife, you're going to have to act macho with us, in any case you would tread along the fence and call out Don Jorge, Don Jorge, and that dear old man would trudge toward our fence, because he was quite old already, approaching you with chocolates in hand, Don Jorge don't give him chocolate or he won't eat his dinner, I would say, ay Leonora just one piece of chocolate, or he would bring you candy, the chewy kind, toffees, I think, and because he was so nice I would say fine, Toñio, eat the candy, those were the days when it occurred to you to sell water for dogs you probably don't remember that, no, Antonio says, I remember I would put leaves in empty cologne bottles, and you would say water for dogs, Antonio's mother says, here the water for dogs, and so the neighbors would stroll by and ask what's in that water, ah, it's a special, magical water to cure street dogs from their sickness, you would say, because there was a lot of street dogs in that neighborhood I don't know if you remember they were all over the streets, dirty and beaten up, we had La Pelusa and La Cuca, I mean La Perla, our unruly street dog, and so it was so funny to see you selling water for dogs, trying to because you never sold a bottle so you would give them away at the end, and so people would tell you okay, can you give me one bottle for the street dogs over there, if you're going to give it to them yes, otherwise you have to pay me, yes, it's for the street dogs over there who are thirsty, and so I would bring out a bowl and we would fill it out with your water for dogs, and so it was this great adventure for you to climb on the fence and hand them the bowl with water for dogs, yes, you and your sister got along very well, playing soccer or hide-and-seek in the patio in that house in Mirandela, that long stretch of patio that culminated in a dilapidated house next to ours, which had a window with what looked like prison bars from where a boy with Down syndrome would watch the two of you play, a boy who must have been eighteen whereas you two were around six or seven at the time, and because I was worried he might say something improper, I was always nearby when he was by his window, shouting out of excitement as he watched the two of you play, and sometimes you would get scared and ask me why does he shout, Mom, and I would say because he's stirred by your games, because he can't play, because he's trapped in that house by himself, why does he have those eyes, Mom, that face, because he was born with a problem and he's always going to be like that, oh so he's sick, you would say, no he isn't sick he just doesn't have a long life ahead of him, but after the three of us finally escaped from that house in Mirandela, Antonio's mother says, I never heard what happened to that boy again.

NOTES TO MY BIOGRAPHER BY ADAM HASLETT

Bureaucracies have trouble thinking clearly, Franklin Caldwell Singer says, I, on the other hand, am perfectly lucid, I, Antonio thinks, am perfectly lucid, too—Franklin Caldwell Singer isn't lucid, Antonio writes, although most of his faculties seem intact—is he also suffused with light?—I am perfectly lucid, too, Antonio's lamp says—and yes, Franklin Caldwell Singer, on his journey to see his son, the only person who meant anything to him—unfortunately some of my children bored me, Franklin Caldwell Singer says, but Graham never did—on his last journey to see his son in a borrowed Saab before he dies, does seem perfectly lucid at first, just as almost twelve months ago Antonio's sister had seemed perfectly lucid when Antonio first appeared unannounced at her house in Baltimore, suspicious he was there, sure, but who wouldn't be if he'd never visited her before, welcoming him to her house and offering him leftover ceviche, her favorite dish with heaps of red onions on top, which he declined because he didn't know how long it had been sitting out on her counter, I already ate, he said, thank you so much—do you remember us eating too many green mangoes in Bogotá, Toñio?—our soured teeth, yes—the bowls of ciruelas and grosellas—and after Antonio settled his bags in his sister's guest room and sat on her couch in her dark living room, his sister, while four split screens on her television tracked the perimeter of her house, as she paced around the subspaces of her living room, approaching the one small window in the kitchen that hadn't been shuttered to yell at her neighbors to leave her alone, told Antonio everything, an everything he likes to believe he doesn't remember anymore just as he likes to believe he doesn't remember the rest of it (when his sister came to see him in Los Angeles one last time, months before she was arrested for allegedly threatening to shoot her neighbors, she brought along photocopies of a military article explaining advanced techniques in mind control, handing them to him and asking for his help—I promised her I would read them, Antonio writes, but I never did, although I remember the diagrams of spy aircraft like geometry assignments—but instead of helping her (what could he have possibly done to help her?) he sobbed in front of her, which didn't help because she stopped telling him anything—I don't want to make you cry, Toñito, Antonio's sister said—), and in her dark living room in Baltimore, as she grew more comfortable with the possibility he was in fact her brother, her everything became a rant that, because of its length and recursiveness, reminded him of Correction by Thomas Bernhard, I know how to appear sane, she said, even if you call the police I know how to appear sane and calm and reasonable, yes, officer, no, officer, that doesn't sound like an adequate explanation of quantum mechanics, officer, laugh, Toñio, that was a joke, when two policemen questioned me yesterday they were impressed at how sane I appeared why would anyone call to report me they can't take me away against my will I haven't done anything, restraining herself from sharing with those two policemen the conspiracies she was sharing with Antonio as she grew more comfortable with the concept of her brother as her audience, Iron Man, she said, radial frequencies from satellites with lasers, covert psychological training, swatting the imaginary insects around her head, are you recording me don't record me let me see your phone, Antonio's sister said, of course I am not recording you, Antonio said, although moments before he had begun recording her in case he needed the evidence as part of the process to commit his sister to a mental institute against her will, and as Antonio rereads

Notes to my Biographer by Adam Haslett, he tries to think about gradations of incoherence in fiction instead of his sister's incoherence in Baltimore, about how in the works of, say, Miquel Bauçà, the lack of linkage between contiguous statements complicates the text—the buttonholes on his shirt more and more match the color of his trousers, Miquel Bauçà says, no doubt this is why his wife has finally been able to sing at the opera house—whereas in Notes to my Biographer the linkage between most contiguous statements contains no complications—the nude dancing incident in the Louvre in a room full of Rubenses was of a piece with other end-of-the-war celebrations at the time, Franklin Caldwell Singer says—in other words Franklin Caldwell Singer, like Antonio's sister, is lucid enough to know you might think his statements might be interpreted as incoherent so he tries to convince you his statements are not incoherent by strengthening the logic of his linkages, and Franklin Caldwell Singer does succeed in planting seeds of doubt about what's sane and what isn't, for instance Antonio could believe in one spy dressed as a reindeer trying to obtain Franklin Caldwell Singer's industrial secrets, but not two spies dressed as reindeers on two separate occasions (Antonio's mother, determined to believe her daughter did not have the disturbance with the horrendous name, would explain to Antonio over the phone why she thought his sister was telling the truth about her coworkers spying on her at home—they've bugged her house, Antonio's mother said, because they knew things we had just talked about at her house—and so his sister started storing all her phones in the freezer, as she'd asked him to do when he arrived at her house in Baltimore), and yes, Antonio did record his sister twice, when he'd first arrived and later that day, after she'd tired of her own rant and he drove with her to dinner at Sí Señor, but no, he will not listen to his recording of her threatening to throw

herself out of his compact rental car or her accusing him of thinking he's better than her because he spent two years at Yale (what
would be the point of transcribing her incoherence in Baltimore?
unlike Adam Haslett, who lightens Franklin Caldwell Singer's incoherence with humor, Antonio cannot yet see the humor in his
sister's fate — why don't you delete the recording then? — listening
to it would be the equivalent of staring at a naked person asleep
on the sidewalk — delete it then —), please, Graham Caldwell
says to his father just as Antonio had said to his sister at Sí Señor,
settle down, no one in this restaurant is spying on us, and while
on the one hand Franklin Caldwell Singer remembers his son
Graham as a child — he used to bring me presents in my study
on the days I was leaving for a trip, Franklin Caldwell Singer
says, and he'd ask me not to go — on the other hand Graham
says to his father I thought my own father was dead, you didn't
call for four years but I couldn't bear to find out, couldn't bear to
go on and find you dead, and so it was like I was a child again,
and here Antonio stops reading, as he always does when he
reaches this passage, unable to continue (of course Antonio
knows why this passage always makes him cry — of course I
know so what? — cry you son of a bitch — Antonio has been pretending his father's dead since Antonio left Bogotá, twenty-four
years ago (Antonio would rather not think about that individual
right now (playing basketball with that individual in his grandmother's patio in preparation for his intramural matches at San
Luis Gonzaga (playing chess with that individual at a second-
rate tennis club while American music played in the background — sailing / takes me away — cry you piece of shit — by a
pool with the tallest diving board he'd ever seen — here are these
memories of that individual what am I supposed to do with
them? — his mother calling him almost a year ago and telling
him that that individual had remarried and his new wife was

accusing him of abusing her teenage daughter from a previous marriage and he was therefore in hiding—I think this is connected to what's happening to your sister, Antonio's mother said, but your sister doesn't want to hear anything to do with him—Antonio finding a way to call that individual who was in hiding to check if he was okay how do you explain that?—children are programmed to be fundamentally loyal to their caregivers, Bessel van der Kolk says, even if children were wronged by them—it's not far down to paradise / at least it's not for me—)))), I can't sleep, Tata, Eva says, let's count bunnies, Antonio says, I tried but they ran away, Eva says, it happens come let's try again together, Antonio says, and after Antonio tucks in Eva he returns to the living room and to Franklin Caldwell Singer and his last journey to see his son before he dies (although Franklin Caldwell Singer never says this is my last journey before I die, if you read Notes to My Biographer as many times as Antonio has, you might also conclude it is the narrator's last journey due to the fact that (1) Franklin Caldwell Singer is seventy-three years old, (2) his road trip includes trying to say goodbye to other family members, who refuse to see him, (3) he has driven from a place where he has nothing left—the eviction notices in Baltimore, he says, the collection agencies—), and after Franklin Caldwell Singer's done exhausting his son with his incoherence just as in Baltimore Antonio's sister had exhausted Antonio with hers, Franklin Caldwell Singer says my son looks so young as he weeps, as he did in the driveway of the old house on the afternoon I taught him to ride a bicycle, the dust from the drive settling on his wetted cheek and damp eyelashes, later to be rinsed in the warm water of the bath as dusk settled over the field and we listened together to the sound of his mother in the kitchen running water, the murmur of the radio, the stillness of evening in the country.

WHEN ARTURO WAS ESTELA

My mother was tired of me biting my sister, Ismene said, and perhaps because she thought I didn't understand biting hurts other people, she bit me in the face, leaving a mark that was embarrassing to explain at school—I like not being seen, Ophelia said, that's why I volunteer at Lighthouse for the Blind—my parents escaped from Laos and spent ten years in a refugee camp in Thailand, Joanna said, and you could tell which members of our family had been born into the camp because they were much shorter due to the food rationing (Joanna told Antonio her grandmother still helps North Koreans escape to Thailand by guiding them through the same trails her parents used to escape, so he asked her to please describe those trails to him, but she had been too little to remember them so he has come to imagine them as the insides of anthills or the dark subterranean passages for birds in the Seuss books he reads to his daughters—Joanna grew up in Kansas, Antonio writes, where she learned about the Flying Spaghetti Monster—dear Flying Spaghetti Monster who definitely exists—Joanna is a marine biologist, Antonio writes, and because of her autoimmune disease she approached our arrangement with abandon, as if sleeping with an unpublished older novelist had been on her do-before-death list—), and as Antonio rereads the few fragments he has managed to jot down from his arrangements so far (most mornings like this morning he's too depleted from his arrangements or from soccer to thoroughly document his arrangements so most memories of them have already vanished from him), he receives a YSA message from Goth Raver, who wants to know if he would like to meet her tonight, and although she does look like a goth raver into psychedelics and bondage, and although it's probably a bad sign that she's not college verified and she has contacted him first even though he has no public photos and she hasn't requested access to his private photos (Antonio likes to believe he has become an expert at filtering arrangements by their photos (if photo = too naked, delete indicator = 1) and by their messages (if first message = I know what I'm worth my exact compensation requirements are $$$, delete indicator = 1)), but of course his filtering system doesn't always perform as coded, or it does but he makes concessions if that week he has no new arrangements in the queue (an arrangement who'd failed both the photo and message filters but was too striking to skip told him she'd been arrested by a policeman who'd posed as an SD so before entering Antonio's apartment complex she asked him if he was with law enforcement because according to her if you are with law enforcement you can't say you aren't), or he'll make concessions if on the same morning he receives a message from both Goth Raver asking him if he would like to be her SD and Ron the Bail Bondsman informing him the private investigator has found his sister in a jail in Milwaukee, and although Antonio would rather exhaust himself at the soccer field tonight, Goth Raver looks so striking in her photos that Antonio agrees to meet her tonight at 9:30 p.m. at Salt Air, and fortunately she looks as striking in person as she does in her photos (unlike his arrangement the previous week who'd claimed to be a poet and a model and turned out to be a tedious tech writer with a cake blog), and so Antonio orders the usual bottle of Cava and the usual tray of oysters and does the usual toast—for not being dead—thinking life is unbelievable and beautiful, unconcerned about the photos with blood coming out of what looks like a knife wound on her chest that she's sharing with him, unconcerned about her

telling him how she'd been approached by a wealthy tech entre-
preneur at the San Francisco airport and how he hired her to be
his secretary on the spot and of course she knew why he hired
her but she was not going to give him what he wanted, and as
usual a black car transports them to The Other Home, where she
undoes the white ankle straps of her stilettos and places them on
his windowsill, which surprises him because most arrangements
who come with stilettos know to leave them on, not that he
minds how on the windowsill the stilettos are facing each other
like spectators who are too shy to look toward his bed, where he's
pecking her feet with his lips, suppressing an impulse to bite her
calves because he's too drunk for the right calculus of teeth, rub-
bing his cheek on her black leather miniskirt as if putting himself to sleep—goodnight cow under the moon—osculating her
thighs that even in the dark he can see have glitter and bruises
on them (he will have to make sure there's no glitter on his face
tomorrow morning—why is your face sparkly, Tata—no it isn't
did you see that platypus over there?—), but as they entangle
each other further, outstretched on his bed, his hands on her
legs, her breath on his neck—the sea / the sea—she jumps up
and informs him she needs to use the bathroom, where she
stays for too long, and when at last she's done he hears her opening his file cabinets in the kitchen but he doesn't rush to ask her
what does she think she's doing because that might sour their
arrangement, and when she returns to the living room she's
holding the card that says I am sorry you hurt your foot Tata
and the photo of his daughters and his former wife that he keeps
hidden on top of his fridge, a card and a photo she drops on the
floor because her hands are jittery, although she doesn't seem to
mind them and of course he's not going to ask her if she injected
herself in his bathroom, motherfucker, she says, as if he's slighted
her somehow, as if someone had pressed a button requesting a

pantomime of horror but she didn't understand the complete instructions, please, Antonio says, calm down, terrified about waking up his neighbors because it's past midnight and she's almost screaming that she needs to leave, don't come near me, motherfucker, she says, even though he's nowhere near her or making any attempt to come near her, order me a car now, she says, and so he, dumbfounded, orders her a car, and she, dredging up more bile, curses at him and conducts an uneven performance of storming out, returning to pick up her stilettos from the windowsill and concluding her uneven performance of storming out, but it isn't over yet because she's still downstairs, screaming so much that Antonio, three floors up, can hear her, so he rushes downstairs and she screams where is my car, motherfucker, please, Antonio says, it's coming, showing her the screen of his phone, which he's holding with both hands in case she tries to snatch it from him, and the trajectory of the Prius on the screen culminates with the Prius picking up this barefoot pantomime of horror, and fortunately there are no neighbors carping at him from their windows, or at least he can't see any of them, but unfortunately it isn't over yet because at 5:30 a.m. she sends him a YSA message saying unless you bring me five thousand dollars by noon I am contacting your wife, who I'm sure will be thrilled to receive screenshots of your YSA profile and photos of me in your foul bathroom, so here it is then, Antonio thinks, at last my turn has come—I don't want to listen to your family constellations conjectures right now—if a family member is ejected from the family system—I'm not your intergenerational if / then puppet—I've always despised plot, Grace Paley says, the absolute line between two points, not for literary reasons but because it takes all hope away—unfortunately my son is not giving himself the opportunity and prefers to follow the path of his father—but I've done nothing wrong, Antonio thinks, unwilling to give in, moreover, I could press charges for extortion, and yet despite having done nothing wrong, if Goth Raver contacts his former wife, his so-called stable family life will be upended, for how will he explain to her the existence of Goth Raver from Your Sugar Arrangements, and so Antonio calls Nicolas, his one college friend, a wealthy Chilean who's also a member of Your Sugar Arrangements but in New York, explaining the Goth Raver backstory and asking him for the name of an attorney, verga, Nicolas says, that's heavy, but how would she even contact Ida did you like lend that raver your phone or tell her your real name, she was going through my stuff and maybe she found my name on one of my utility bills in the kitchen or maybe she did a reverse photo search online, Antonio says, mira, Nicolas says, my friend is an immigration attorney but what you need is a criminal attorney let me ask my friend for a referral but text me a photo of Goth Raver or no deal ha ha, and while Antonio waits for a referral from Nicolas, Antonio tries to contain his panic because it's 9:30 a.m. already — breathe, motherfucker — no, he will not wait for Nicolas, who has always been unreliable in any case, he will search online for a criminal attorney with good reviews, and once he finds one that can see him at 10:30 a.m., he cancels his meetings at Prudential Investments and rushes to meet this random criminal attorney he found on the internet, are you sure you didn't do anything to her, the criminal attorney says, you have to trust me and tell me the truth or I can't help you, nothing, Antonio says, showing the criminal attorney her photos and her messages, Goth Raver, the criminal attorney says, examining her photos as if they were assignments from a class on American pornography, I know, Antonio says, has she contacted you again, the criminal attorney says, yes she texted me at 9:45 a.m., Antonio says, showing him a message that says I know you read my message on the site if you don't deliver the money by noon expect to see me and my boyfriend at your doorstep, and so what I want to know, Antonio says, is whether I should press charges for extortion before she contacts Ida or wait to see if she's bluffing, and clearly the random criminal attorney from the internet doesn't know the answer because he says let me check with my colleagues, calling one colleague, two colleagues, okay, the criminal attorney says, we don't want to alert the police since she might be bluffing, so don't press charges, stay put, print her photos and messages, place them in a folder with a note I will write for you and carry this folder with you at all times, pay me two thousand now and two thousand later, that way you're protected if she contacts your family or if the police have to get involved, but Antonio decides to wait before signing any contracts because Nicolas has finally messaged him a referral, and so he leaves the office of the random criminal attorney from the internet and calls Nicolas's referral, explains the extortion backstory, and the referral says she's too busy for his case so she refers him to another criminal attorney, who has time to meet him in two days, meanwhile, the random criminal attorney from the internet messages him to say on second thought I need the full four thousand now, which confirms Antonio's suspicions that the random criminal attorney from the internet is trying to scam him, meanwhile, back at his desk at Prudential Investments, it's 12:00 already, 12:05, 12:10, but his phone doesn't ring, 1:30, 1:45, but he receives no YSA messages from Goth Raver, no texts, but what if Goth Raver and her boyfriend are already waiting outside my apartment, Antonio thinks, so that night he decides to sleep at the apartment where his daughters live, as he's allowed to do three times a week at most, standing by the window of his former wife's bedroom to check if there's any strange cars outside his apartment, three doors down, why are you standing by the window, Tata, Ada says, I am waiting for the Flying Spaghetti Monster, Antonio says, let's play Monster, Ada says, who can tell me which Dr. Seuss book contains underground tunnels for birds, Antonio says, oh I know, Ada says, running to the living room and returning with I Had Trouble in Getting to Solla Sollew, which he has read to Ada and Eva many times before, read it, Tata, Eva says, I Had Trouble in Getting to Solla Sollew by Sandra Boynton, Antonio says, come on, Tata, I Had Trouble in Getting to Solla Sollew by Dr. Seuss, I was real happy and carefree and young and I lived in a place called the Valley of Vung, Antonio reads, and nothing, not anything ever went wrong, is he a cat, Tata, Eva says, an invented Seuss creature I think, Antonio says, he looks like a cat, Eva says, no kitten around, Ada says, and the Seuss kitten escapes from the Poozers by jumping into Vent #5, well, that vent where he went was sort of a funnel, Antonio reads, that led him down into a frightful black tunnel, with billions of absurd birds clogging the tunnel with tubas, skateboards, cactus, look, Tata, Eva says, the fish from The Cat in the Hat, I was down there three days in that bird-filled-up place, Antonio reads, and the next day Antonio avoids his apartment again, unable to sleep because what if his former wife receives a message from Goth Raver and decides he shouldn't be allowed to see his daughters again or what if his daughters open his backpack and unearth the Goth Raver Extortion folder he has been carrying with him at all times, until at last he's sitting in front of the criminal attorney referred to him by Nicolas's referral, I represent thieves, he says, arsonists, murderers, what the hell are you doing here, so Antonio shares the Goth Raver backstory and hands him the folder, Goth Raver, he says, examining her photos as if they're part of an art project he's expected to admire (he does), I know, Antonio says, I hear about these scammers on these sugar daddy websites all the time have you heard from her again, he says, no, Antonio says, and you won't, he says, if you haven't heard from her by now you won't hear from her, there's nothing for me to do here, be more careful next time, don't take them to your apartment because if they see you have a nice apartment they will be more tempted to scam you — my extra-small studio apartment is a filthy nook, Antonio doesn't say — and make sure they're over eighteen because I've encountered cases where they organize group sex sessions and sneak in an underage girl for extortion purposes as well, now get the hell out of my office, the criminal attorney says, handing back Antonio's folder, I have criminals to represent, and so Antonio exits the criminal attorney's office, wondering where he should hide the folder he has been carrying at all times, and how long he should keep it (just in case), and whether he will keep his promise to quit his beloved website later today (perhaps tomorrow?).

Soccer as science fiction, Antonio thinks—science fiction for people who don't read science fiction, Silvina would have countered since Antonio hasn't read much science fiction besides A Lexicon of Terror & Other Stories—soccer as A Lexicon of Terror, Antonio thinks, soccer as science fiction culled from interplanetary war films I used to watch with my father at Cine Los Mayas, soccer as a transport between worlds such that, if soccer indicator = 1, for instance, then location = Bogotá and Los Angeles and time = 1989 and 2014, which, sure, isn't that remarkable, anyone in Los Angeles who possesses even one vivid memory of another city can be in two places / time periods at the same time, but perhaps it would be more remarkable if he adds a discontinuity indicator to factor in the twenty-one-year interlude when he didn't play soccer, in other words if he, after arriving to the United States, age eighteen, would have continued to play soccer every day as he had done in Bogotá, irrupting into the spaces between his classmates on the dusty soccer field at San Luis Gonzaga as if someone had disinterred his undead and he, without knowing it, was both escaping them and squelching them—pass the ball already, Bruja—accumulating red cards and releasing a sizable fraction of the thermodynamic violence apportioned to him by his upbringing, he probably wouldn't be equating soccer with science fiction while running SQL queries at Prudential Investments and waiting for news of his sister, in other words if discontinuity indicator = 0, then soccer <> science fiction, but unfortunately for the discontinuity indicator to ever equal zero he would have to have been a different Antonio, because that version of Antonio (henceforth Antonio II), age eighteen, had reprogrammed himself to complete his one assignment, to be admitted to an Ivy League, so Antonio II spent most of his time either solving differential equations for transferrable math courses, which didn't require him to compute the language, or listening to transmissions of American English at the ESL lab at his community college south of Chapel Hill, learning to compute a new language he liked to believe he knew but didn't—you also wanted to gain muscle weight at the gym since you were as scrawny as a—that's neither here nor—you quit soccer because it made you lose muscle weight, you vain fuck—yes and later you stopped watching soccer on television because you wanted to think of yourself as an intellectual ha ha—so given that discontinuity indicator = 1, then soccer = science fiction, location = Bogotá and Los Angeles, and time = 1989 and 2014, and yes, what he'd said to Dora about the soccer linkage between Ada and him was true—as if I was watching an apparition of myself as a boy playing soccer in Bogotá but much better, Dora—but what he hadn't told Dora is that after Antonio VII (father of Ada & Eva) watched Ada on the soccer field, Antonio IV (intellectual) felt a longing to transport himself twenty-one years back and set the discontinuity indicator for Antonio II (Ivy League) and Antonio III (bodybuilder) to zero, and because that wasn't possible he purchased soccer cleats, shin guards, expensive jerseys from a Spanish team he didn't know, and transported himself to a pickup soccer game in Los Angeles, where he discovered, within minutes, that discontinuity or continuity or whatever, time had indeed passed and Antonio IX (old man soccer) could neither run for long nor maintain possession of the ball—why are you even here, nerdo?—and what had been remarkable to Antonio VIII (writer) was how, despite a span of twenty-one years, Antonio IX (old man soccer) couldn't disconnect himself from Antonio I (young man soccer), and so as Antonio V (database analyst) creates a spreadsheet to tabulate the other Antonios, linking Antonio IX and Antonio I with a Curved Double Arrow Connector, he's reminded of the essay about the overweight psychotherapy patient who discovered that, as she was losing significant portions of her weight, memories of her life when she last had that weight came back to her — as if my body has a memory, she said to Dr. Irvin Yalom — yes, Antonio thinks, his own body not only has a memory but two twisted ankles due to the irresponsible equivalence of Antonio IX = Antonio I, his left ankle, incidentally, hasn't recovered so a chronic pain appears and disappears in it depending on the weather, time of day, etc., and just as Antonio VII and Antonio VIII and Antonio V had agreed to shut down Antonio IX to avoid further physical injury, his sister began to ununderstand her life, so all the Antonios still in operation reconvened and agreed that, instead of reactivating temporary disruptive erasure mechanisms like binge drinking or nightclubbing in order to not think about what was happening to his sister (and here Antonio omits Your Sugar Arrangements from his inventory of temporary disruptive erasure mechanisms — déjenme por lo menos un joy, carajo —), they decided to call off the shutdown of Antonio IX, allowing him to recalibrate himself by (1) following the instructions of how-to-tape-your-ankles videos, (2) studying the less taxing passing strategies of Modrić and Iniesta in midfield, (3) not following the instructions of how-to-stretch-before-and-after-a-soccer-match videos because stretching reminded him of his mother's yoga classes in the forest and made him feel old, and once the recalibration had been completed, he began to not think about his sister while chasing a stupid ball for an hour and a half, and despite the sports tape on his ankles and the Epsom salt baths afterward and restricting the wrecking of his body to twice a week, he exists in a constant state of strain now, beginning with his left toe, which cramps on him for no discernible reason, his left thigh, which requires a thigh sleeve while he's reenacting a recalibrated Antonio I—there are turns and feints that only occur while stamping across a soccer field, Antonio writes, and perhaps because these movements are otherwise dormant they electrify everything when they reawaken—this new state of strain, paradoxically, at the same time (1) assuages him, (2) extirpates (most of) his impulse to sink himself with his sister, (3) aerates the subspace corridor that links him to his sister, wherever she might be, okay, 5:01 p.m., folks, enough with the SQL queries and the nebulous science fiction associations (last week one of his classmates at San Luis Gonzaga posted a recent photo of Cine Los Mayas, where he used to watch interplanetary war films with his father on Sundays, its windows and ticket booth boarded up), so Antonio removes his oversized circumaural Sennheiser headphones, which have been transmitting Phase Patterns by Steve Reich on repeat, switches off the fluorescence of his cubicle—goodnight, Lucid—rides his Shadow VLX from the Prudential Investments building to the apartment where his daughters live, thinking along the way of the futility of the bodybuilding efforts of Antonio III since Antonio IX has now lost so much muscle weight due to this new recalibrated soccer that he's almost as scrawny as he was at twenty-one years old, and after dinner with Ada and Eva and his former wife—no dinner for me thanks I have soccer tonight—you should have told me I wouldn't have fried the steka yet, monkey—he stretches out his body on the living room floor so he can wrap his ankles with a layer of self-adhesive bandage and multiple layers of sports tape, those are my scissors but you can borrow them, Eva says, can I come watch you, Tata, Ada says, they have no school tomorrow, Ida

says, of course, Antonio says, so Antonio transports Ada and
Antonio IX to a turf field on Woodbine Avenue, where Antonio
tries not to think about the message he received from his sister's
attorney informing him that his sister is finally being transported from Milwaukee to Baltimore through an interstate police system that doesn't allow him to know her precise location
yet but instead tries to focus on scoring, passing, skirting
opponents, including an oversized college student who clearly
doesn't know anything about soccer because whenever Antonio
has the ball he just barges against Antonio as if the ball be-
longed to this giant and Antonio was just a nuisance to be
shrugged off, and perhaps because this amorphous giant reminds him of El Mono, a classmate at San Luis Gonzaga who
resembled an orangutan (and who used to beat up Antonio
whenever), Antonio becomes flustered, irrationally angry, and
when this awkward blob dispossesses him again by interposing
himself between Antonio and the stupid ball, Antonio pushes
him so hard that this primate piece of shit falls backward, quit
fouling me, motherfucker, Antonio says (later Antonio will
consider that if he would have had his metal water bottle handy,
he would have smashed it against this guy's face), I call the fouls,
the organizer of the pickup game says, we don't do violence
here, we don't want people like you here, you're out, but he's
been fouling me all night, Antonio says, embarrassed as he exits
the field because he'd forgotten Ada was watching him, what
happened, Tata, Ada says, that moron kept fouling me, Antonio
says, they should have kicked him out, Ada says, that mnemo-
cartographic dunce, Antonio says, trying to lighten the mood
on their drive back to where his former wife will shake her head
at him — no milk for you, little boy — that wocket in the pocket,
Ada says, that zelf under the shelf, Antonio says, do you believe
in ghosts, Ada says, no nobody has seen them, Antonio says, the

caretaker at this church told us that it was built over a cemetery and they have footage of ghosts, Ada says, we would have heard, Antonio says, ghosts are like Jesus or god, made up, imagine if I say I'm going to invent a strange creature called Snæborg Ocampo, and then I say oh but Snæborg Ocampo is invisible, ah, Ada says, I understand, we humans have a need to believe someone is watching over us, Antonio says, but there is someone watching over me, Tata, Ada says, you and Mama.

ANTONIO'S MOTHER BY NICOLA CARATI

Your grandmother Martina didn't talk about her upbringing, Antonio's mother says, instead she would repeat the same refrain that her mother died when she was a small child so she had to live with her father, what other refrains do you remember hearing from my grandmother, Antonio says, asking his mother about his grandmother from his father's side during Christmas #6 because Antonio was trying to insert the voices of his grandmothers into a novel set in Bogotá, recording his mother while his former wife and his two daughters tried to sleep in his mother's guest room in Sioux Falls, rewinding his 1:46:43 recording of his mother and listening to her saying your grandmother Martina didn't talk about her upbringing, just as neither Antonio's sister nor Antonio ever talked about their upbringing, drawing flowcharts of his mother's associations in his 1:46:43 recording of her as winter #8 comes to an end without news of when and how his sister will be transferred from Milwaukee to Baltimore, tracing his mother's shifts from one anecdote to another, starting with Martina, the ice cream enterprises of her brother Lucho, the humorless enterprises of her brother Francisco, Lucho's wife saying to Lucho you're going to change or you're going to change because I'm not divorcing you, her brother Francisco who calls her now that his family is also falling apart, all of it in the first 19:28 of his 1:46:43 recording of his mother sitting across from him at her dining table during Christmas #6, his daughters sneaking into the living room to pirouette for them like child actors performing the role of daughters who, like his own daughters, had already attended dance performances choreographed by Merce Cun-

ningham, Sasha Waltz, Martha Graham—my favorite was the
dancer with the metal wings going rarr rarr, Tata—the phone
not ringing in his mother's kitchen with news of his sister, who
before Christmas #6 had severed all communications with his
mother after she'd conjoined reality and irreality for the first
time, in other words this was his mother's first Christmas in
Sioux Falls without his sister either there in person or calling her twice a day, the imaginary Christmas lights flickering
on his mother's Christmas tree while he recorded his mother
talking about her own upbringing, yes, he can invent Christmas lights flickering behind them and he can invent a family
trip on Christmas Eve to a Mormon temple where hundreds of
teenagers listened to a handful of teenagers onstage strumming
about the lord their savior, but this kind of invention equates
to a noninvention because during Christmas #6 his mother
had indeed decorated a Christmas tree with flickering lights,
and they did take a family trip downtown where they chanced
upon a teenage Mormon temple, he just didn't think of either
while listening to his recording of his mother at work until he
wondered whether he would need to describe the setting of his
recording session if he were to write about it, as he's planning
to do whenever he's able to write again, or describe the days
before and after he recorded his mother during Christmas #6
in Sioux Falls, where his mother still lives with her American husband, and as Antonio listens to his recording of his
mother, he decides to prolong his time with his mother's voice
by (1) drawing flowcharts of her associations, (2) transcribing
her recording in the original Spanish, (3) translating his transcription of her recording, (4) calling his mother after steps (1)
to (3), although unfortunately these calls probably won't last
1:46:43 but less than 1:00.

—

None of us wanted to play cards with my brother Lucho, Antonio's mother says, except yes he would convince me, late at night during the school break he would tiptoe to my room, at midnight he would knock on my door, Leonorcita, he would say, Leonorcita, yes what's the matter, let's play cards, he would say, no because you're going to cheat and then we'll fight and then Mom and Dad will punish us, I promise you I won't cheat, he would say, and so he would come into my room and we would play cards, but with money, he would say, how old were you, Antonio says, eight or nine perhaps, and so when I didn't have money, we're talking cents here, I would say I can't play with money I don't have any money and he would say don't worry I will lend you some, and if you win, you return it to me, and if you lose, you owe me for next time, no I don't have any money, and he would hand me five cents and say there you are so you can play, and I knew he was going to win because he always cheated so I would ask him to stand up and of course he'd hidden cards on the side of his shirt, he was an artist when it came to tricking me so he could win, and in the end of course we would quarrel, you're a cheater you're always cheating, don't shout, he would say, don't shout, until Mom and Dad would discover us and fiiiit, they would send us to bed, but before leaving my room he would attempt to charge me, remember I lent you this much and now you owe me this much, he would say, no I already told you no, and later yes, he would rent his comic books, but not so that he could then buy chocolate for the poor, as my mother told you, but because Lucho loved money, all his enterprises were so that he could amass money, everything he did was so that he could have more money, even if he accumulated it little by little, that was part of the fun for him, he'd always been that way, I know because I was the one who spent the most time with him and he always wanted me to join his enterprises like for instance he convinced me to make ice cream with him so we could sell it, but without Dad finding out because he'd forbidden us, and so Lucho would say okay but you have to contribute to the investment for the materials, for the coconut, for the, well, Mom would give us the milk and the sugar but the coconut yes, we had to buy it, and so we were supposed to invest half and half, and so we would make the ice cream, place it in the freezer, and then we would tell the kids in the neighborhood that we had ice cream but to not come when Dad was in the house, but sometimes Dad would park inside the garage so the kids didn't know Dad was home and they would come and call out ice cream, señorita, and Dad would admonish us but later he would forget and we would restart our business, and Lucho would do the accounting for every ice cream, how many we'd made, how many we'd eaten, and if we'd eaten any he would try to charge us, although between me and him we were allowed one per day, but of course we would eat more than one per day, and so Lucho would chase me and my brothers around the house trying to charge us for the ice cream we'd eaten, yes, Lucho was something else, Antonio's mother says, and as Antonio translates his transcription of his mother he remembers playing cards at a tournament with his uncle Lucho at the Colombian Social Club in Miami, which consisted of a converted garage in an alley, playing cards as a team when Antonio was fifteen or fourteen and his uncle Lucho flashing him severe looks whenever Antonio would bungle his hand because goddamn it he should have known those cards had shown up already, flashing him severe looks that Antonio must have enjoyed because, unlike the severe looks of his father, Antonio knew they weren't a prelude to him being kicked or shouted at but that afterward his uncle Lucho would guffaw with him about winning, losing, not drinking again during tournaments, and so when it was time to share the ice cream earnings Lucho would say no you're in debt with me, Antonio's mother says, you ate too many ice creams so we don't have any earnings left, all the earnings Lucho would take for himself, but with him it was always amusing, always he's been funny and inventive and charming, and so I didn't join his ventures for the money but to spend time with him, to share these moments with him and he's still the one that calls me the most, when he heard what was happening to your sister he called me immediately and he checks on me every week, the rest of your uncles don't like to bring it up.

—

God will punish you, my mother would say, the lord said that what you inflict on your mother and father will return to you fivefold, so now you know what awaits you in life, my god what's going to happen to me, I would say, what will I have to endure later in life, everything magnified through a child's imagination, of course, if I'd said to my mother, for instance, I am running away from this house because I can't stand it here anymore because my parents are unjust, and my mother would reply your words will be punished by god because a son or a daughter can't say this to her parents, and later the nightmares I would have my god what's going to happen to me, what will I have to endure later in life, and I would try to find in the bible where it said that I was going to be punished and I couldn't find it, but my mother always invoked divine retribution whenever we did something wrong because hers was a religion of torture, of punishment, not of spirituality, that's what I remember the most from being a child my mother accusing me, pointing with her finger at everything that awaited me as a consequence of my actions, her voice trailing off so Antonio rewinds his recording of his mother and tries to soothe her as if she's his own child—sana sana / culito de rana—don't worry Mom god doesn't exist he won't punish you for trying to run away from your house just like I tried to run away from yours when I was your age—rewinding his recording of his mother to trace what had prompted his mother to begin talking about divine retribution, right, okay, his question to his mother had been what refrains do you remember hearing from your mother when you were growing up, which was the same question he'd asked her about his father's mother because Antonio had been trying to insert the voices of his grandmothers into a novel set in Bogotá, and as he listens to his mother saying that god will punish you, that the lord said that what you inflict on your mother and father will return to you fivefold, he wonders how his own daughters would answer the same question about refrains, worrying that perhaps their answer would be just as bleak—Tata always said either way we're all going to die—yes but Mama ordered him to stop saying that so he snipped his refrain to either way we're all going to—or Tata would sometimes say don't forget to bring a towel, which years later we found out was a refrain from a pot smoking character called Towelie in an asinine cartoon show called South Park—but no, Antonio will not worry for too long about their answers because tonight, as his tasks as a database analyst come to an end for the day, he will record his daughters and ask them what expressions do they think they will remember from growing up with their mother and father, starting with Eva, what I don't get it, Eva says, what will you remember your Mom saying to you, that she always loves me, Eva says, no the kind of things she would say to you, that she loves me, Eva says, what else, that she will never go away, Eva says, what about funny things, once she said Tata eats like a pig, Eva says, okay what about phrases Tata says to you that you will remember, that he loves me, Eva says, what else, another thing that's super funny is when you say Mama's butt is base, Eva says, and that's it, his recording of his youngest daughter Eva lasts 4:13, and as Antonio rewinds his recording of Eva he wonders if she's simply too young to understand what it means to remember the past, to blur, avoid, recast aspects of the past — what child would believe you if you told her that forty years into the future her head will carry thousands of vague voices at the same time? — and perhaps if someone would have asked Antonio as a child what expressions do you think you will remember from growing up with your mother and father, Antonio would have never guessed that his answer, forty years into the future, would be I don't remember any expressions from either my mother or father — I love how many times you've said my Mom had an expression, Stephen Colbert says to Vice President Biden — remember nobody is better than you, Vice President Biden says, but you are not better than anyone — and then Antonio records Ada, who says, in response to the question about expressions she will remember from her mother, Ada no, Ada says, what else, Ada sem, Ada says, what else, Ada můžeš sem na chvíli přijít, Ada says, what does that mean, Ada can you come here for a second, Ada says, what else, Ada můžeš sem na chvíli přijít, Ada says, what does that mean, Ada come clean your room, Ada says, what else, Ada come eat the phone is on the plate, or Ada stop it, or Ada go brush your teeth, that's all I can think of — I never say come eat the phone is on the plate that's what my mother used to say to me, Antonio's former wife messages him — what does it mean, Antonio says — it doesn't translate well it's like saying there's a phone call waiting for you at the table why are you asking all these questions, Antonio's former wife says — and unfortunately Antonio tells his former wife about his question and Ada's quotidian answers to his question and his former wife texts him a sad emoji and stops responding to his texts, refusing to tell him how to transcribe the last three Czech phrases Ada had said to him, okay now the same question but about your father, Antonio says, gooooool, Ada says, what else, go score some goals today, Ada says, what else, cut cut cut, Ada says (Antonio has hired a private soccer coach for Ada, an Italian coach who likes to say cut cut cut with a heavy Italian accent, meaning cut to the right, cut to the left to skirt defenders), you sing a lot of songs, Ada says, what else, Eva come play the game with us, Ada says, what else, Mamo where are my glasses, Ada says, Mamo where are my quarters, snoring we took a video of you snoring, snoring is not a refrain, Antonio says, I know, Ada says, perrito / perrito / perrito pierninuska, or move up, move up you say that a lot when I play soccer, what else, you have to use your body when you're defending, Ada says, you think you will remember these when you grow up, Antonio says, definitively, Ada says, okay let's forget about expressions and think about moments, Antonio says, you are playing with Perrito and Perrito pees, or you're going to the bathroom and you go tpppppft, or you are drawing numbers on my back before going to sleep, or you are reading me a bookie, or you are slapping Mama's butt, or you're looking for your glasses, for your quarters, for your keys, when I took the money from the table, but I didn't yell at you for that, Antonio says, because you would be mad at me and that was after the time you said that if I don't get good grades you will ground me that was mean, Ada says, what else, what I will also remember for the rest of my life is my first goal and the car going beep beep beep after the ball went through the goalie and hit that car, Ada says, and unfortunately Ada's erasures are already happening, Antonio thinks, because during dinner a few weeks ago Ada had accused him of not attending her soccer games and his former wife had to intervene and correct her by saying no, Ada, your father has only missed two games ever because he was out of town due to his job, and Antonio had to remind Ada of being there when she was four and she scored her first goal and the car going beep beep beep, which is probably the reason why she brought up her first goal when he asked her about moments she will remember from growing up with her father.

—

We barely saw Dad, Antonio's mother says, sometimes we only saw him on Sunday afternoons because he worked a lot, though we would share moments with him here and there, he would call home at around nine, nine thirty to say he was coming and so all of us would sit around the table to share with him that moment when he was going to have dinner, and so he would order, well, it was already known that a huge slab of meat had to be prepared for him, a platter of meat with rice and lentils, and he would cut us a piece of meat and feed it to us, no we already ate, we would say, open your mouth and eat, he would say, because he had this notion that in order for us to grow we had to eat meat otherwise we weren't going to grow, and he would say to save money your mother doesn't give you enough meat, which was true, and so Dad would buy meat and would feed each one of us to make sure we ate meat, yes, at home we had abundant food, that was the main preoccupation, but it was true my mother would put some money aside to buy herself jewelry that she would never wear because either the maids stole it or something would happen because the jewelry would disappear, and so Dad figured it out so he decided to start buying the meat, which was the only food item he would buy himself, well, meat but also cheese from Cúcuta, his home-town in Norte de Santander, and so he would come home with his cheese and those tasty square crackers from La Universal, and so we had to sit around him at the table, each one of us had to eat a slice of meat that he would feed to us like birds, a slice of meat plus the square crackers with cheese from Cúcuta, and Mom would say but they already brushed their teeth, Víctor, they can brush their teeth again, he would say, open your mouths, eat, there you have cheese and a glass of milk, but we already ate, Dad, we're full, bah, at this hour you must have digested your food already, because we would eat at six, six thirty, and here Antonio rewinds his recording of his mother because this is his favorite part, his gruff grandfather feeding meat to his mother, to Uncle Francisco, Lucho, Hernán, Víctor Roberto, his gruff grandfather who changed everyone's life by becoming an American citizen and providing green cards for his children and his children's children — your grandfather memorized the English dictionary and studied day and night so he could pass the medical exam in North Carolina, Antonio's mother said — who paid for Antonio's plane ticket to New Haven because Antonio couldn't even afford a plane ticket from Chapel Hill to New Haven, and Mom would say but they already brushed their teeth, Víctor, Antonio's mother says, well they can brush their teeth again, open your mouths, eat, and Mom had us trained and would say don't take away food from your father he arrives tired from work, but we don't take anything from him he gives it to us, no, open your mouth, my dad would say, and he would feed us one by one, so we would eat and finish the square crackers, okay, it's late and you have to wake up early, so we would go to our room, yes, that was the part of the day we had to share with Dad, that was sacred to us, for Dad it was sacred, in other words we couldn't skip it, everyone come sit down, he would say, and we would all come to the table to be with him.

—

Dad was addicted to stress, Antonio's mother says, in other words he would function better under stress, and so in the morning during the week Mom would start with her recitation of Víctor, Víctor, it's 7:25 already, your daughter has to be at school at 7:30, which was a problem because from our house to the school it was twelve or fifteen minutes by car, but Dad would leave at 7:25 and I would say my god we're not going to make it, this is so embarrassing the nuns are going to reprimand me again, every morning the same story, bah, you don't have to worry I will speak to the nuns, my dad would say, and so he would sit me in the car and he would say okay now hold on, there was no safety belts back then, hold on, and we would speed out of the house all the way to Maria Auxiliadora, my elementary school, hold on, he would say, and he would speed us there, because he always liked to speed, running red lights, yellow lights, and when he would see a red light he would look on one side, on the other, and he would say hold on and zoom us through, and so I would hold on and go zssssisst with the wind on my face, and the nuns would reprimand him, of course, and he would appease them by bringing them medicines, by offering them free medical consultations, yes, tomorrow I will come on time, madrecita, you know that I'm busy, but why don't you just put her on the school bus so the girl doesn't have any more problems, yes, madrecita, tomorrow, madrecita, until finally I would cry and say I am not going to school I am too embarrassed of always being late, and so eventually I was allowed to go in the school bus, but that was years later when I was in sixth grade, and here Antonio pauses his recording of his mother, closes his eyes and sees his mother and his grandfather speeding across Bogotá—grandpa?—yes what want do you want I don't have any money—I understand now why you wanted to drive my mother every day that was your special time with her—good for you go water your fertile imagination elsewhere and leave me alone—do I remind you of you?—you're studious like I was, sure—I see an umbilical cord like a fire hose connecting you and me across the universe—stop reading your mother's quack therapy recipes and go back to your database job—and so my Mom would say Víctor, it's 7:25 already, Víctor, it's 7:20 already, all right woman I know leave me alone, every morning the same story, let me finish my coffee, you already had like four, Víctor, goddamn it why do you have to be counting my coffees you're not the one having them, from when he would open his eyes he would drink his coffee, black and concentrated in espresso cups, and he would drink the last coffee on his way to the car so the domestics had the coffee ready for him at the door, here's your coffee, Dr. Hernández, and it was all a pretext, later I understood it, because when he worked here in the United States it was the same story, he had to be at work at eight in the morning and if it would take him fifteen minutes to get there he would leave ten minutes prior, and so he would have to speed there, because he was addicted to stress, that's when I understood it, but Mom was like a clock, every morning repeating Víctor you're going to be late, Víctor, they were like cats and dogs, that was their dynamic, that's how they courted each other, that's how they fell in love, how they married, how they raised seven children, and that's how they lived until Dad died.

—

You can't live here anymore, Dad said, you can't continue to disrespect the rules of this house, your siblings, your mother, you've been given many opportunities but you've refused to change, and so Dad expelled my brother Víctor Roberto from the house, and yet despite our fights with Víctor Roberto, because yes he was always inciting us and fighting with us, plus he was the only one who would dare talk back to Dad, we missed him, our oldest brother, when is he coming back, we would say, when is Víctor Roberto coming back, and Víctor Roberto hasn't forgiven us because he felt that he was expelled from the family, when what he needed at the time was help from us, but in those days psychological help just wasn't something families sought out, I think he started doing drugs and his personality started to change, although he was always hyperactive, extremely intelligent but inconstant in his pursuits, he knew he was intelligent but he wouldn't put his intelligence into practice (and here Antonio makes a note to ask his mother more details about Víctor Roberto's pursuits because he vaguely remembers hearing over the years that Víctor Roberto either piloted jet planes or designed jet planes or rockets but was thrown out of the military for misconduct (and here Antonio decides not to pursue a potential linkage between Víctor Roberto being expelled from everywhere and his own history of being thrown out of his elementary school, his high school, his former apartment where he used to live with Ada and Eva and his former wife, thrown out of so many places that Antonio has wondered if that's the only way he feels most at ease, and what he also remembers about Víctor Roberto is that the domestic at the apartment where Antonio lived with his mother had instructions not to let Víctor Roberto in if his mother wasn't there, and years later, when his grandfather, Dr. Víctor Hernández, died in Chapel Hill, North Carolina—goodbye Grandpa, thank you for everything—Víctor Roberto flew to Chapel Hill and apparently checkbooks and important papers from his last will and testament disappeared in his wake)), and so Víctor Roberto had a lot problems with Francisco, Antonio's mother says, because Francisco was the perfect son, and Mom would always compare between Francisco and Víctor Roberto, Dad never compared between us but Mom did, because for Mom Francisco was a reflection of her Italian side of the family, oh so you're the perfect child, Víctor Roberto would say, you're the blue blood, and so they would fight each other all the time, and by the time they became adolescents these fights became frightening, and Mom couldn't control them anymore because they were men now, and I know Víctor Roberto thinks we were relieved when he was gone but that wasn't the case because we missed him, he was our oldest brother, he would occupy the corner of the dining table, next to Mom at the head of the table, as the oldest he would sit next to her and the rest of us would have to accommodate ourselves whichever way, and so to always see him in that seat, which Francisco occupied after Víctor Roberto left, no, we would say, Francisco shouldn't be sitting there, that's always going to be Víctor Roberto's place, I was always the one fighting about it and I would tell Mom don't allow Francisco to sit there that's Víctor Roberto's place, Víctor Roberto isn't here anymore, Mom would say, he isn't here now but he's going to come back, I would say, and Mom wouldn't say anything and Francisco continued to occupy Víctor Roberto's place, which I felt was an injustice, and later when I studied constellation therapy I learned that when someone is excluded from the family system, the family system undergoes a distortion (and here Antonio decides to order books on constellation therapy to check if they yield any associative threads of interest, although the titles of Bert Hellinger's constellation books (Laws of Healing, Love's Hidden Symmetry, Looking Into the Souls of Children) grate on him, a cynical Colombian with a penchant for being thrown out of everywhere), even more if Francisco took over Víctor Roberto's place, as if Víctor Roberto didn't exist anymore, as if Francisco had become the most important, yes, Francisco did feel he'd become the most important in the family, and that Víctor Roberto wasn't there anymore was a great sadness for us because as a family we were really close, all of us during lunch, dinner, vacations, and all of a sudden he was gone, and to this day Víctor Roberto hasn't escaped this state of feeling rejected, of feeling we all rejected him, to this day he speaks as if we all rejected him, and so I think this was a great sorrow for my Mom but she couldn't deal with him alone, she needed help from Dad but because Dad worked so much he couldn't be at home more often, and so that was the only option Dad had, to throw Víctor Roberto out, and because Dad had come from studying in the United States where children leave the house when they turn eighteen, perhaps he felt it was okay, but in Bogotá this wasn't part of our tradition, children left the house when they married, and so I think life marked him, to me this marked Víctor Roberto, who was the smartest one of us, to this day he continues just as irresponsible, complaining and blaming us for his misfortunes, never coming through in life.

—

I did fall in love with somebody else, Dad said, but my family was more important, I wasn't going to allow my children to be unhappy, to live far away from me, and for me that was more important than the person I'd met, and I don't regret it because I had you near me, and it hurts me that your mother somehow felt it, although I don't think she ever found out, she must have felt that I had found someone else, and as Antonio rewinds his recording of his mother he wonders if his mother was recasting this anecdote about her father, turning it into a moral tale of familial love and sacrifice and so on to remind him of his responsibilities as a father, and yet he doesn't call her to ask her about this anecdote because he barely talks to his mother, hasn't called her on any of his (1) to (3) cycles as he had imagined he would do when he started listening to his recording of her, has barely talked to his mother since the time when he decided to leave his former wife and his mother sided with his former wife, who at the time was pregnant with Eva, and of course in retrospect he can see that his mother was right, he should have ignored his misgivings about being a father again and stayed with his former wife while she was pregnant, but six years ago, and this he hasn't forgotten, the feeling of being trapped in a life he hadn't chosen overwhelmed any consideration about a child he didn't yet know (and here Antonio searches for the emails his mother had intended for his former wife back then but inadvertently sent to him instead—even though my son is a great father to Ada with his attitude he is losing his rights to be a father of the new baby, his mother wrote, unfortunately my son is not giving himself the opportunity and prefers to follow the path of his father—no, Antonio thinks, he can't stand to read these emails again, they are still too painful), and so I asked Dad if he fell in love with someone else when he came to the United States to study, Antonio's mother says, yes, Dad said, but why does that time come to mind, because when you came back you would play romantic songs, and I was very little, I must have been five, four and a half, and I remember you would play a song called el reloj—reloj / detén / tu camino—Dad had brought back a record player and music, in those days it wasn't common yet to have a record player, and he would play that one record over and over, he would arrive home and to relax he would play that song, and later, when I was much older, I would sing that song, and he would say to me oh shut up already you're out of tune, and I would say let me sing I sing because I like the song, no, no, you're out of tune quiet down, I never heard him sing again, only that one song back then, when I was so little still.

—

I wrote Dad a letter, Antonio's mother says, after that surgery on his pancreas when he almost died I wrote him a letter telling him that he'd been given an opportunity to change his life, that he could have been gone just like that, that all that money he'd amassed he wasn't going to be able to take with him, and that it was about time that he share with us what he felt, who he really was, and when he was at the hospital, for a month he was at that hospital, he would ask my mother to read him my letter every day, read me my daughter's letter, he would say, and she would read it to him and tears would pour out, and from then on he changed, in the last fifteen years he had left after that surgery to his pancreas he became more loving, more worried about his grandchildren and his children, he would call me three, four times a day when I came to live in the United States, he became more worried about us, I mean, it wasn't all about him anymore, he was more worried about others, and that's how he began to help everyone, and if someone in the family needed anything, he would give it to them, and your sister when she called your uncle Luis, who still manages Dad's inheritance, your sister told him my grandfather says that if he was alive he would have helped me, because she was calling to ask Luis for a donation when she had to stop working due to her condition, and so in her desperation she would tell Luis that she was speaking to your grandfather and that your grandfather told her he would have helped her if he was alive, and this was true, Antonio, he would have helped her.

—

My grandmother the nurse quarreling with my grandfather the doctor on the stairs of a hospital in Bogotá before they even had their first lunch together, Antonio thinks on his way home from his database analyst job at Prudential Investments, my grandfather Víctor saying to my grandmother Remedios I already found out your name what kind of parent calls his daughter Remedios, my grandmother saying to my grandfather I am not moving to the United States how can you expect me to leave half of my children here, a nurse telling my grandmother to please not leave Dr. Víctor alone in the United States because there's another woman who's trying to steal him from her, my grandmother saying to the teenagers who bag groceries at her local supermarket in Chapel Hill, North Carolina, moo, leche, because she didn't know how to say milk in English yet (Antonio's mother laughing as she tries to imitate her mother saying moo, leche—you weren't embarrassed that they didn't understand you I would have been so embarrassed, Mom—bah tarados who don't know Spanish they should at least know the meaning of leche—), my grandfather the surgeon phoning my grandmother the mother of seven children to say he was coming home and everyone rushing to clean the house because he was a militant man of sanitation, inspecting everything to make sure it was in order when he arrived home, my mother saying your grandmother never spoke ill of your grandfather despite his bad temper and his numerous flaws, we never thought of our father in negative terms that was just our life, how we coexisted with Dad (the summer before starting college Antonio lived with Grandpa the surgeon and Grandma the housewife and Grandpa would yell at Antonio for playing his music too loud and Grandma would yell at him for not washing the blender after making his protein shakes and on Saturday mornings Grandma would wake up early and drive to the garage sales in the neighborhood, proudly bringing back an ancient bowling bag for Antonio, for instance, and because he was still a teenager Antonio would put on his headphones and not talk to his grandmother for days, or until she issued him an ultimatum (Antonio likes to believe he learned English by watching Jerry Lewis marathons on his grandparents' television)), my mother not including in her narrative that because of what her parents were like she decided against moving to the United States with them, finding an excuse to stay in Bogotá by marrying a man she barely knew, a man with whom she would have two children, Antonio and Estela, who would both grow up to prefer that this man didn't exist, who have severed all contact with this man so as to pretend he doesn't exist (Estela when she was eleven, Antonio when he was eighteen), and as Antonio arrives at the apartment where his daughters live he's resigned to the possibility of encountering this man in his sleep again, as he has done for more than twenty years, although in his sleep Antonio doesn't play basketball with him on his grandmother's patio, as he had done with this man, nor does Antonio play chess with him at a second-rate tennis club on Sundays, as he had done with this man, nor does he watch interplanetary war movies at Cine Los Mayas, no, in his sleep the scarred lunar landscape and the catastrophe around him is always the same, or at least he prefers to remember it in this vague one-version way instead of as an accretion of variations on the same impulse, he hasn't written down any of his encounters with this man so as to make them less concrete, more forgettable, and although he can't recall anymore if his first encounter with this man in his sleep frightened him twenty years ago, by now his encounters with him have become yet another image he has to contend with, in other words while he's awake, if he happens to remember his encounters with this man on a scarred lunar landscape, he isn't frightened or traumatized or saddened, absolutely not, one can get used to anything (except to watching The Exorcist), and even if he knows there's likely a correlation between the brutality of his encounters with this man while he's asleep and his outbursts while he's awake, what is he to do except hope none of these outbursts overturn his life irreversibly, and perhaps this is one of the reasons he has begun playing soccer again after not playing soccer for twenty years, because he has always associated soccer with violence, the mad sprints on the wings, the unhinged tackles, the name calling, the red cards thrown back at the referee's face, and perhaps soccer not only depletes him of the energy that fuels his violent outbursts but brings him back to those years in Bogotá when he would propel himself down the soccer field every day while his sister was discovering that when she was little the man known as her father had committed repugnant acts against her that would roil her life and her reason despite her attempts to pretend this man didn't exist, and as Antonio falls asleep he's resigned at experiencing the terror that comes with his encounters with this man, yes, just because he's used to these encounters doesn't mean he doesn't still experience terror, terror like in those horror films he doesn't watch because why would he want to feed material to the landscape around his encounters with this man—feed your violence, you swine—terror like when he witnesses what he does to this man in that scarred lunar landscape, the man approaching him, an ax in Antonio's hand.

TIME PASSES BY VIRGINIA WOOLF

The wind, Antonio reads, sent its spies about the house again, they're summoning you in the other room, Ida says, numbers, Ada says, sparkling water with ice, Eva says, what power could now prevent the insensibility of nature, Antonio says [in a mock horror voice], lights off, Ida says, one more page, Mamo, Antonio says, this side, Perrito, Ida says, my side of the covers has all the amenities plus free lectures on literature, Mister Perro, Antonio says, if he chooses your side of the bed there will be chicken drumsticks for dinner for a week, Ida says, but what after all is one night, Virginia Woolf says, why are you doing this to me, Antonio's father says, say to your son I am not afraid of you, Peter Ström says, your phone contains a recording of your sister, Arturo says, don't need to hear it, Antonio says, open your iTalk app and press aaaa, Arturo says, leave him alone his visit to his sister's house in Baltimore has been erased already, Antonio's mother says, the red button on your iTalk app that says aaaa, Arturo says, your tooth implant looks beautiful the bone has regenerated, Dr. Sze says, your sister has been delivered to Baltimore City jail in Baltimore, Thomas Saville says, we're waiting for her to be transferred to the Spring Grove State Hospital in Catonsville, Maryland, 3:16 a.m., Antonio's phone says, no chance of falling sleeping again, Arturo says, but the stillness and the brightness of the day were as strange as the chaos and tumult of the night, Virginia Woolf says, here's the living room where Ada used to dance to Ravel's Une barque sur l'océan, Nicola says, running across it in her pink ballet uniform, Dr. Adler says, the Blood Bank out the window, Hershleder says, two men loading plasma into a truck, Katerina says, a truck that will traverse a valley that will resemble the X-rays of your tooth implant, Arturo says, Bovary's multilayered hat according to Nabokov, Jules Jakobsdóttir says, that vent where he went was sort of a funnel, Dora says, that led him down into a frightful black tunnel, did my mother send you to ogle me do you want café con leche, Estela says, or do you want to rest first or rent a movie to distract yourself, what movie do you want to see, Antonio says, Iron Man we can buy it at Best Buy, why don't we rent instead of buy, Antonio says, I want to see it on the television screen, can't you connect the computer to the television, Antonio says, yes but I need the cables, what cables, Antonio says, you know what cables don't be a moron, I wouldn't know I don't have a television, Antonio says, yes you do you hide it from your daughters, I don't have a television, Antonio says, the one in the closet in Ida's room, ah that old mammoth I threw it away already, Antonio says, see I remember everything I'm not crazy the government says that the technology in Iron Man equals the technology deployed through (sorry for the interruption) satellites Barack Obama says that if we [in a robotic voice] don't. leave. this. filthy. house, and don't tell me it isn't a filthy house there's radial frequencies from satellites with lasers that come from the solar system in other words the sun therefore there's abundant vegetation as in a neighborhood park due to the abundant solar energy therefore there's forest animals also, how many hours a day does Barack talk to you, Antonio says, twenty-four hours a day Barack isn't the one who talks to me the CIA talks to me from the Pentagon which controls the armed forces Barack is the leader of the government that controls the CIA they're doing to Obama what they're doing to me sorry. for. the. interruption, which means he's a CIA trainee which means that (stop looking at me sexually) you have to have psychological training from your sister so you can feel better about yourself otherwise Ida and my mother are going to shred you psychologically, they called from Robert Half they're about to cancel your temp contract you will lose your health insurance so we need to talk to them, Antonio says, I'm sorry I'm the one who needs to talk to them it's as if the CEO of Prudential Investments had made a mistake you report to the CEO of Prudential Investments, no, Antonio says, don't tell me that who do you report to, I work in a group called sales and marketing headed by Morton Stephenson, Antonio says, why are you lying to me, why would I lie to you, Antonio says, you don't speak to the CEO every now and then, no, Antonio says, he doesn't call you Guatemalan Superstar yes he calls you Guatemalan Superstar if he doesn't do it to your face he does it behind your back because it's a joke by Barack Obama, if there's no medical certificate justifying your extended medical leave they will cancel your temp contract, Antonio says, I abandoned my job because I have four felony charges pending and according to the instructions given to me by the American government I can't return to work because the client is a media company that has invaded my phone and chases me through the radial system in my car those pieces of shit charge eighty-four dollars an hour for me imagine the margins that's why Robert Half hasn't thrown me out yet this is privileged information (don't interrupt me) if you tell that bitch of my mother I will deny it because there's no invoice to prove it you're quite smart to be working at an investment firm so they can't invade your personal life because it would affect the Federal Reserve System of the United States, they called and said unless you provide them with a medical certificate they're going to cancel your contract, Antonio says, I don't have a certificate I have a legal issue that I can't comment about, I understand but if you don't talk to them they will cancel your contract, Antonio says, if I go back and talk to them and say I have legal issues pending the manager will say what legal issues and I will have to tell her I can't talk about it so she will run a background check on me and she will find out I have four felony charges pending and Robert Half will share it with all their clients so what my lawyer is doing (let me finish) he's saying (no, you're in my house, and I adore you, Toñito, but this is the first time you've been here, and I thank you that you're here) but my lawyer is doing the same thing your CEO is doing to your marriage he's not giving you a raise because you've made the wrong decisions he will spy on you and they will steal your psychiatric files they will know your psychological problems caused by that bitch of a mother by the lies and bribes of Ida who impregnated herself for money they're going to say if you're so smart with your two years at Yale we want to see how you come out of this problem now if you betray me and say to Robert Half [in a little girl's voice] my sister has four felony charges and I am a moron who works for the CEO of Prudential Investments and I travel to the Federal Reserve and I've seen all the hot women in Baltimore and my sister when she's fit she's more beautiful than any stripper from the Gold Club and more intelligent than any of the strippers from the Gold Club and because I am a moron I allowed myself to be taken in by Ida who's the biggest criminal in the world because there's rumors she killed her grandmother I am Antonio Jose Jiménez I am a moron who allowed himself to be conned by my mother who's a bitch [in an angry voice] who sucked my dick when I was an adolescent to destroy me for the rest of my life you think my mother didn't touch me inappropriately when I was little and I don't remember she touched me inappropriately and left me on the floor, naked, yes, my mother, and the American government blocked it from me they're so advanced in their military technology they blocked my brain I had forgotten until now that I'm stuck here in this filthy house receiving secret information from the American government I sound crazy I know it sounds crazy because they're so advanced nobody can believe it so they recommend that we see Iron Man because it isn't a technology invented by Iron Man but by the American government I hope you understand the logic and don't think I'm crazy because the logic of my legal situation (sorry. for. the. interruption) is what I do need you to understand and why I can't call Robert Half do you understand why, no, Antonio says, your logic has limits, or you're tired, stop looking at me sexually, you filthy rat stop looking at me sexually I call you filthy rat not to insult you but because you've lived like a filthy rat being the best father in the world that's why they've promoted you like the filthy rat that is Ida who has abused you psychologically like my mother, the problem with Robert Half, Antonio says, is that without their contract you won't have health insurance and that's a considerable problem, I don't need to see a doctor and you can threaten me a thousand times that you're going to commit me to a psychiatric institute but as long as the police find me sane they can't commit me to a psychiatric facility, and what happens if they don't find you sane, Antonio says, my lawyer has the medical records I am not crazy I just have mood swings, nobody is saying you're crazy what did your lawyer say about it, Antonio says, stop patronizing me, I'm asking you a question because I need to understand, Antonio says, why are you here is it because my mother has nothing else to do or because you want to talk about your divorce with Ida, why would I want to talk about my divorce with Ida, Antonio says, because you have to divorce her otherwise you will never get promoted they're going to steal your psychiatric exams and they're going to see you're a moron that allowed his mother to suck his dick and nobody defends him why doesn't anyone defend him because they're jealous that you're handsome and intelligent and because we come from a racist family, why did your lawyer call 911, Antonio says, because he was drunk the police felt bad I sent him a text saying if the rest of the Guatemalans called him to please not answer the phone he said calm down we'll talk next week he's a nice guy, why would a nice guy call 911 on you, Antonio says, because he had enough of my antics he knows I'm normal why didn't the police take me to a psychiatric institution it's a mind game until you catch up to the big leagues, bro, you're not going to get it, what's going to happen if someone else calls 911 if you're being antic at the supermarket for instance, Antonio says, you said antic, that's the word you used, Antonio says, psychological antics like what I'm doing to you right now, I'm concerned about your current state, Antonio says, why are you concerned, I'm concerned that you are having, Antonio says, that you are in a situation that you are not well, please leave this instant I hope it goes well for you I can throw you out of my own house, I know you can throw me out, Antonio says, why don't you leave then, why would I leave I'm giving you my opinion, Antonio says, you can go now, I am not going, Antonio says, leave or I'll call 911 so they can remove you, call 911, Antonio says, if you start behaving like my mother I won't tolerate it you will leave the house I will call the police, I don't know what you mean, Antonio says, do you want to go out and eat something, yes I'm hungry, Antonio says, stop crying as well, I'm not crying, Antonio says, stop crying the worst that can happen is that I lose my lawyer I can get a court appointed lawyer I can retrieve my psychological files Obama is tired of your psychological antics and says that if you don't believe me that he protected you while you were at Yale and you're a moron who believes my mother who sent you that means you're letting yourself be manipulated by my mother which means you can leave my house (sorry for the interruption) I don't want to suck my mother's vagina or lick my father's penis for the rest of my life that's why I prefer to be alone I say this metaphorically you know I haven't seen my father since I was eleven he barely did anything to me but because my mother is a crazy perverted woman that was raped by her brother she comes here to screw us up and my father barely shouted at me and he hit you and my mother sucked you so you will have the same psychological problems as her for the rest of your life the government blocked it from me so I wouldn't be traumatized unlike you who's a man and if you don't want to believe me that the government can do it, don't believe me, that's your problem, you will end up an embittered old man, alone, I am a spy for the American government that's why they can't take me to a psychiatric facility, let's take a time-out, Antonio says, I've overwhelmed you already, yes, Antonio says, speak, the Censor says, for you have summoned me, I don't want to remember any of this, Antonio says, you misunderstand the nature of my role, the Censor says, the Censor censors, Stanley Elkin says, I disguise, the Censor says, not erase, disguise as blanks, Antonio says, up to you what the disguise will be and not up to you do you understand, the Censor says, is this your first day of high school too, Antonio says, yes but I'm already in the honors program, Silvina says, me too, Antonio says, coincidence, Silvina says, that strange machine, open your iTalk app and press delete, Arturo says, aaaaaaaa, Dr. Sze says, through the open window the voice of the beauty of the world came murmuring, Virginia Woolf says, too softly to hear exactly what it said, el panadero, the ambulatory salesman says, la vitamina.

WHEN ANTONIO'S MOTHER STAYED

After I confronted your father, Antonio's mother says, he ran to
his parents and acted like he was the victim, and his parents,
who were like my second parents, sided against me, claiming
that I was slandering him, and that how could I possibly believe
what a child was saying, but your aunt Sofía called me and said
Leonora I have to tell you something, because I wasn't well, Antonio, and here Antonio pauses the recording, unable to continue, trying to compose himself because in less than an hour
he has to playact at being a database analyst instead of a novelist
who insists on spending his mornings listening to recordings of
his mother as he awaits news of his sister, composing himself as
he recalls his mother, drained of life, seeing her own body on
the sofa from above and feeling a pull toward the light, a con-
soling light, Antonio's mother had said to him when he was still
a child, a peaceful light, a light that over the years he has interpreted as god, as the light at the end of the tunnel from the New
Age death literature, peace at last, etc. — out-of-body experi-
ences can be induced by delivering mild electric currents to the
temporal parietal junction in the brain, Bessel van der Kolk
says — as the outcome of the electric currents Antonio's grandparents were inflicting on his mother by pretending his sister
was lying, and as I was ready to leave this world, Antonio's
mother says, because I wasn't well, Antonio, I'd become a skel-
eton by then, my face was covered in boils, I remembered the
school bus would be dropping off you and your sister soon, and
so I panicked because who would open the door for you, who
would take care of you if I was gone (for years Antonio has been
seeing the ghost of his mother battling to return to her drained

body so she could open the door for them, for years Antonio has not thought about the ghost of his mother until today (and because he's a parent now, has been one for eight years, he's on the one hand relieved that he can see himself emulating his mother in that moment, and on the other hand he suspects that if he were to discover someone had been harming his daughters in his own home, he wouldn't feel a pull toward any goddamn light, he would simply abdicate reason and knife the culprit)), when did you confront that individual, Antonio hears himself say in the recording, when we were still living in that house in Mirandela, Antonio's mother says, that's strange because my sister told me years later, Antonio says, when we were already living at that other apartment, yes she told you because a sexual education class at school reminded her, Antonio's mother says, oh so she told you beforehand, Antonio says, yes what happened is that she blocked it out, Antonio's mother says, and how could she not since your father accused your sister of being a liar, you're demented and so is your daughter, he would say, and your sister would hear it and she would say I'm not crazy, Mom, no, Estelita, I believe you, I am going to defend you, I know what could have been happening, and it pains me that I wasn't more alert, and from then on, as soon as she told me, I began to sleep in your room, I was there with both of you, all the time, and he would tell me you have to come back to our bedroom, no, I am not moving from here, you're never touching our daughter again — why did you keep us in that house with that individual, Antonio didn't ask his mother while he recorded her — please don't ask me that question haven't I had enough punishments already? — yes, no — and so when his parents sided against me, claiming I was slandering him, Antonio's mother says, your aunt Sofía called me and said I never told you because my parents forbade me to do so, Leonora, but my brother touched us improperly, all three sisters, and instead of finding help for him my father thrashed him and sent him away to military school, that's why my youngest sister Lucía can't stand him, you've seen how Lucía treats him, whenever he tries to hug her she screams, so I do believe you, Leonora, and you haven't reminded your parents about this, I said to your aunt Sofía, yes but you know my mother has always been blinded by her love for my brother and my father does whatever my Mom says, but I want you to stay calm because I know you're telling the truth, and if you have to take drastic measures, take them, so I confronted your father again and told him what Sofía had said and this became another scandal with his parents because why did Sofía have to interfere, his parents who were like my parents, Antonio, who disheartened me because I respected them, loved them, when I was pregnant with your sister they asked me to live with them so they could take care of me because my parents were already in Chapel Hill, and so after this new confrontation your grandmother Martina paid for us to see a psychiatrist, who did tests and asked for drawings and said well, perhaps the child imagined it, I don't see anything concrete in these drawings, perhaps the child invented it, I think the best thing to do is for me to help you, because this is too traumatic for you, he said, plus your husband doesn't want to come anymore since he says he's not the one who has a problem, and then this psychiatrist tried to take advantage of me, on top of everything I was going through this psychiatrist abused his role, what was his name, Antonio says, Winston Villamar, Antonio's mother says — dear Winston Villamar, Antonio writes, if you aren't already dead, you son of a bitch, I wish one day you and everyone you know will read my mother's words — I had to run away from his office, Antonio's mother says, and later he called me and said that I couldn't prove anything, that no one was going to believe me, and of course I never returned to his office but for a while he would lurk near the house in his car, he was the most famous evangelical pastor in Bogotá, that's why your grandmother Martina picked him, your grandmother Martina who never accepted what your father did, Antonio, who would come over to visit you and your sister at our new apartment, bringing sweets and acting as affectionate as possible, but whenever I would leave to the other room she would start saying things to your sister, and one day I heard her from the other room saying what you're accusing your dad of isn't true, this accusation stems from your mother not being right in the head and we are thinking of pressing charges so they can intern her in a psychiatric facility for crazy people, and if you continue to accuse your father you're also going to that facility, and so when I heard this, Antonio, I ran over and threw her out, you don't step in this house ever again, I said, I am here to defend my children, I believe what has been happening, and if you ever want to see them again it'll be under my supervision, I am never leaving you alone with my children, leave this house this instant, and so your grandmother stopped coming, whereas your grandfather would secretly stop by and bring you sweets, and later your grandmother would tell me bring the children to me, please, and I would say I'm sorry but I am not taking them to you, you've caused my daughter too much harm, because they should have supported her, Antonio, nobody in that family supported her, and when years later your grandmother Martina was gravely ill, when you and your sister were already here in the United States, I was meditating alone in my yoga studio and your grandmother appeared to me and said forgive me, Leonora, and I said to her I have already forgiven you—dear Grandma, Antonio writes, I haven't forgotten you, I still remember my summers in Cartagena with you, the tiny mallet you would carry in your purse because you loved to eat crab legs by the beach, I still remember you and Grandpa stationed on the beach under your parasol while my cousin Leonidas and I boogie boarded all day, and even though I don't remember you threatening my sister, don't remember much about those years, no, Grandma, I don't forgive you—but your grandmother insisted, Antonio's mother says, please forgive me, Leonora, she said, everything has been forgiven, I said, wondering if perhaps your grandmother's health had deteriorated further, and about fifteen minutes later your father called and said my mother just died and she never had a chance to talk to you because you never came to see her, yes, your grandmother was gravely ill but I did not visit her—I left Colombia when I was eighteen, Antonio writes, and I never saw those horrible people again—so I said to your father I already said goodbye and she asked me to forgive her, how is that possible, he said, she appeared to me, I said, bah, he said, and he hung up the phone, I do remember when my aunt Elena came to exorcise my sister, Antonio says, yes and your sister couldn't sleep for months—Aunt Elena, Antonio writes, you knew what my father had done to you and your sisters and you had the nerve to come exorcise my sister so she would stop accusing him?—your sister would sleep in my room because your aunt Elena had terrorized her, your aunt Elena, who I had to forbid from visiting the two of you as well, and just imagine, Antonio, when your sister started feeling unwell in Baltimore, when she was still working at Fidelity Insurance as a Senior Actuarial Associate and couldn't sleep—more than thirty years later, Antonio writes—she didn't want to seek help because she was worried that they were going to intern her in a psychiatric facility, that they were going to tell her she was crazy.

THE BYSTANDER BY GINA BERRIAULT

Someone shouted at me to grab a blanket or a coat or something for crissakes, the narrator of The Bystander says, and wrap your old man up, because after assaulting the woman the narrator's father liked best, and after running out with nothing on but the soap from the bath he'd been taking with her, the narrator's father is standing on the street, shouting imprecations at her, and although Antonio never remembers the exact phrases that describe what happens next (The Bystander by Gina Berriault first appeared in Antonio's life as a reading assignment during a retrograde narrative workshop, almost twelve years ago, before he'd met Dora or Silvina or his former wife, before his sister began to ununderstand her life (what had drawn him to The Bystander and other fictions of ununderstanding if no such condition had afflicted anyone he knew back then? If Antonio were a conspiracy theorist, which he isn't, he would suspect that someone had been planting these fictions near him to warn him or prepare him for his sister's misfortunes — I am not a conspiracy theorist, Antonio writes, and fiction doesn't prepare you for anything — hi Nicola — shut up —)), he hasn't forgotten the terrifying image of people watching the narrator's father from windows and balconies, of people at a bar nearby, laughing at the narrator's father, and perhaps Antonio hasn't forgotten this terrifying image because of its familiar dream logic, all of a sudden you find yourself on the street, without clothes, and people are laughing at you (and here Antonio searches for his copy of The Unconsoled by Kazuo Ishiguro, which does not yield any associative threads of interest — the dream logic of The Unconsoled is calibrated to be logical and illogical at the same time, Antonio writes—), but to the narrator of The Bystander, who tries to cover his father with a blanket—he struck me away with his elbow, Antonio reads, sharp in my ribs as a crowbar—the dream doesn't end with the people laughing at his father or with his father being taken away by the police, no, he, the son, still has to visit his father at a mental institute—your grandmother Martina claimed your father's forceps delivery at birth impacted his head, Antonio's mother said—and because Antonio has been hearing about this forceps theory for years he searches online for forceps + birth, hoping to debunk his dead grandmother's exculpatory theory—although rare, the Mayo Clinic says, risks to your baby include minor facial injuries due to the pressure of the forceps, minor external eye trauma, skull fracture, bleeding within the skull, seizures—I brought his suitcase, the narrator of The Bystander says, as the young man social worker had told me in some huge loft of hundreds of desks and social workers in an agency building that was probably not unlike the agency building where Antonio and his mother filled out the forms required to process their request for an involuntary inpatient treatment for his sister, announcing his and his mother's dark purpose at the designated window, sitting apart from each other in the waiting room, a young man leading them to a bare room where he explained to Antonio and his mother the procedure, one form for his mother, one form for Antonio even though in the state of Maryland only one written testimony was required to commit his sister to a mental institute, his mother objecting to her son's use of the word schizophrenia in his testimony, him and his mother wavering at the question on whether the person they were trying to commit to a mental institute was at risk of self-harm, Antonio proofreading his mother's lengthy testimony—her words, Antonio writes, completely erased from me—my daughter wrote beautiful letters, Antonio's mother said—nodding his head, trying to appear reasonable—I was leaning my elbow on the counter, the narrator of The Bystander says, smoking a cigarette, demonstrating with that pose my reasonable nature—and if at that moment, when Antonio and his mother were done filling out the forms required to commit his sister to a mental institute, a butterfly would have landed on him or his mother, they would have burst from grief, but no butterfly came so Antonio and his mother continued as before, containing their organs inside their bodies, waiting for the young man social worker in silence, a silence they maintained throughout the morning and afternoon, as if afraid the most innocuous word might weaken their resolve to commit his sister to a mental institute—butterfly—let's not do this anymore—a resolve that originated mostly from Antonio, who, because he thought he needed to be a man of action, had decided they should take control of his sister's circumstances—her dangerous isolation, Antonio writes, which could have aggravated her legal situation—and since his mother had been too exhausted to object, here they were, waiting for the young man social worker, who returned to the bare room and apologetically explained what would happen next, don't worry, he said, she won't be able to read what you've written on the forms and the police will inform you before they're on their way to her house (but of course later the police didn't inform them and they did show his sister what they'd written on the forms), and so they exited the agency building as quietly as they'd entered it, searching for his compact rental car, heads down, focusing on their steps so as to avoid falling flat against the asphalt—like Henri in A Christmas Tale with Catherine Deneuve, Antonio writes—over my arm I carried his raincoat and in my pocket his wallet, the narrator of The Bystander says, containing, under celluloid, a snap-

shot of my mother taken the year before she died and a snapshot
of myself at the age of five, and as Antonio rereads The Bystander in the living room of the apartment where his daughters
live, his former wife asks him what's wrong, Antonio, any news
about your sister, and instead of telling his former wife that
while performing his database analyst tasks at Prudential Investments earlier in the day his sister's attorney had called him
to inform him that at last his sister had been transferred from
Baltimore City jail to the Spring Grove State Hospital in Catonsville, Maryland, where she would remain until she was
deemed fit to continue her trial proceedings, he asks his former
wife to please read The Bystander out loud to him, no, she says,
I need to prepare your daughters' school lunch for tomorrow,
okay, he says, but she takes pity on him and reads to him in the
kitchen about Arty, the son, who's visiting his father at the mental institute, the impact of his presence in this alien place made
my throat swell, his former wife reads, and I went up to him
quickly and laid my hand on his back, the smell of oranges was
on his breath, his former wife reads, and that was good, I
thought, his former wife reads, if he had eaten an orange then
he was comparatively content, what do you think they'll do to
me, Arty, his former wife reads, Tata, Antonio's youngest
daughter says, numbers, Eva go back to bed it's late, his former
wife says, I'll be there in a second, Antonio says, you tell them
in the psycho ward they give your father hot chocolate and a
little cookie, his former wife reads, why are you reading this, his
former wife doesn't say, and perhaps because his former wife is
crying he says I'll go do numbers before it's too late, me first,
Eva says, that's not fair, Ada says, I'll flip a coin heads or tails,
head, no, tails, here it goes, let me see turn on the light, Ada
says, head wins so Eva goes first, fifty numbers today, Tata, just
ten, twenty-one, can you sing cuando vuelva a tu lado, cuando

vuelva a tu lado / y este solo contigo, and once Antonio is done drawing numbers on both of his daughters' backs and singing a song from Eydie Gormé y Los Panchos, he returns to the kitchen, I'm going to bed, his former wife says, so she turns off the light in the kitchen and living room and goes to bed, but Antonio remains in the living room, trying not to think about butterflies, agency buildings, forms filled with tenebrous words, let's drive to your sister's house to make sure she didn't forget to lock up, Antonio's mother said after his sister had been apprehended, I don't want to I'm scared she might still be there, Antonio didn't say to his mother (on the second day of his unannounced visit to his sister in Baltimore, she'd stormed into the guest room where he'd been updating his mother on his sister's condition over the phone and his sister screamed at him to get the hell out of her house (after he switched on his compact rental car and the air conditioner started running, he couldn't hear his sister anymore but she was there, guarding her driveway and screaming at him, her new imaginary enemy, her last family connection)), and so after Antonio called the police department and someone informed him that yes, the deed authorized by him and his mother had been done, his mother insisted they drive to his sister's house, and so they did, parking in his sister's driveway, where the motion-detection light clarified the existence of his sister's house for them, but Antonio did not want to roll down the windows or step out to check if all the doors of his sister's house were locked because what if his sister was still there, waiting to hurl herself at them like the undead, and so the motion-detection light, registering no further motion, expired, and so they remained inside his compact rental car in his sister's driveway, terrified, and so Antonio switches on the lamp in the living room of the apartment where his daughters live and searches for his copy of A Questionable

Shape by Bennett Sims, which he doesn't find in the bookshelves nearby so he switches off the lamp and powers on the flashlight on his phone and searches for A Questionable Shape on the bookshelves in the bedroom where his former wife is already asleep, nothing, so he searches in his daughters' room and finds A Questionable Shape on Ada's bookshelves, yes, he'd forgotten that, during a long holiday weekend, they'd played the game of Can Ada Read the First Page of Whatever Book Tata Picks, A Questionable Shape by Bennett Sims being one of the books Antonio had picked—what we know about the undead so far is this, Ada had read, they return to the familiar—they'll wander to nostalgically charged sites from their former lives, Antonio reads, and you can somewhat reliably find an undead in the same places you might have found her beforehand—and Ada and Antonio had both laughed as Ada tried to read the word mnemocartography—this book contains so many beautiful words, Antonio said—what are you doing, Tata, don't take my platypus again, Ada says, bookie expedition go back to sleep Bunnytown, Antonio says, returning to the living room and thinking that instead of that horrible word his mother had objected to he should invent beautiful words to describe his sister's illness, even though there was nothing beautiful about his sister's illness—from your point of view, bobito—yes, look at these beautiful words from A Questionable Shape, which he'd penciled on its title page, apophatic, for instance, which means to describe something by stating characteristics it does not have—my sister's house did not have a television in her living room with four split screens tracking the perimeter of her house—yes it did—aphasia, for instance, which means inability to comprehend and form language because of a dysfunction in specific brain regions, and which, incidentally, is also the name of a piece of invented nonsense sign language by Mark

Applebaum—dear Mark Applebaum, Antonio jots down on the back of A Questionable Shape, I want to omit myself from the surface of this world by learning to perform Aphasia—Aphasia is a metaphor for expressive paralysis, Mark Applebaum said—when I was in high school I was possessed by an unexplainable fury, Antonio had written months ago on the title page of A Questionable Shape, and it is all coming back to me now—it started around the time my sister was arrested for the first time, Antonio thinks as he angles the flashlight of his phone on the last page of The Bystander by Gina Berriault, the son turning around and seeing his father standing by the window of the mental institute, watching his son go, and I knew then that I was guilty of something and he was accusing me of it, Antonio reads, and it was the guilt of sight, for he was the father who breaks down under the eyes of his son, the father in his last years when all the circumstances of his life have got him trussed and dying, while the son stands and watches the end of the struggle and then walks away to catch a streetcar.

WHEN ANTONIO & ESTELA DIDN'T ESCAPE

After we escaped from that house in Mirandela, Antonio's mother says, your father would drive by our new apartment, and if he didn't see your uncle Lucho's jeep outside, he would ring the doorbell and try to force himself inside, yelling, with the authority he thought he had as a man, you are my wife, these are my children, and on one occasion, when the two of you went with him, that was so ignorant of me, Antonio, that was a mistake, Estela has to come with me because she's my daughter, he would say, and still, I shouldn't have allowed it, but, well, she'd told me what had happened with your father, and since the psychiatrist had said there was no information and I didn't want to probe her too much on whether it was true or not, I protected her though, we are leaving this house, I said, I protected both of you, because you were just as impacted as she was by his screams and his violence, and so on one occasion when we were already living in our new apartment, he came to see both of you — my father reading stories to my sister and me in the living room in that apartment is that memory possible? — yes, no — and he took both of you for the first time, and when your sister came back home she was crying and trembling and she said I don't want to go with that man ever again, Mom, I am afraid of him, and so then she told me he'd slapped her and she had tried to throw herself out of the car, but Estelita something could have happened to you why would you do something like that, because he said he was going to kill both of us so I screamed no, no, and he said he was going to smash the car against a wall, you don't remember, no I don't remember, Antonio says, you were probably in the back seat, I am not leaving you with your mother, he'd said, we are all going to die together, and he began to accelerate his car, and that's when Estela started crying and screaming and he slapped her face, and so she opened the door and tried to throw herself out, and with me she felt the same way, Antonio, when I would drive her to work on the freeway in Baltimore, and here Antonio pauses the recording, unable to continue, closing his eyes and thinking of his sister's trajectory since she left Colombia when she was eighteen (studying actuarial science at the University of North Carolina, working as a Senior Actuarial Associate in Charlotte, Mexico City, Baltimore, visiting him in Los Angeles for his twenty-seventh birthday, buying a house, crashing her car on the freeway one rainy evening on her way back from work, soon after grandfather Víctor passed away—your sister always felt your grandfather was the only one in the family who supported her, Antonio—), and as Antonio takes inventory of how little he knows about his sister's adult life, he wonders if, just as his sister buried what had happened to her, he has buried her along with what happened to her, and if this was the case—of course this is the case how else do you expect me to function day after day?—how can he expect himself to help his sister, or rather, sure, he can expect himself to be a decent human being and help his sister, but then (and here he sees himself driving a truck at night and falling asleep at the wheel after hours of driving and then awakening in a sunny garden—wake up, Antonio—) his habit of burying her would take over and he would bury her and her troubles, wake up, Tata, but perhaps listening to these recordings of his mother every morning is his way to remain alert to his sister's misfortunes—how are we to remain awake to the misfortunates of the world without sinking ourselves?—and so Antonio opens his eyes and rewinds his mother's recording and she's saying with me she felt the same way, Antonio, when I would drive her to work on the freeway in Baltimore, and she would tell me Mom you're driving too fast, I am not driving that fast, Estelita, no Mom too fast, stop, stop, I can't stop here we're on the freeway, I'm going to jump out of the car, calm down, please, we're getting off the freeway right now, when was this, Antonio says, when she had already had that incident with her neighbors and she was arrested for the first time, when I stayed for months with her in her house in Baltimore and I would drive her to work using only city streets, she couldn't handle the speed of the freeway, Antonio, and that day I had told her look, there isn't that much traffic on the freeway, we'll get there faster, but then unfortunately we hit a zone where cars were racing by and I had to follow the speed of the other cars, and that's when she became desperate, I had to grab her and say no, no, no, Estela, you're staying in the car, we are going to get off the freeway right now, and so from then on we only drove on city streets, and so in retrospect I can of course see that she was reliving the trauma that she had lived through with your father, and that the magnitude of what had happened that night in Baltimore with her neighbors, the violence of it all, because one of the women who accused her had tried to run her over, and she wasn't able to defend herself, Antonio, and the cops treated your sister like a criminal, handcuffing her while searching her house for weapons, and so this precipitated a return of those events of abuse and aggression that she had buried for years, and when she told me what happened with your father on that occasion that the two of you went with him in his car for the first time, I told him over my dead body you take the girl with you ever again, you don't take them out, either of them, but he tried through the law to take you with him, because he was embarrassed that if neither of his children wanted to see him what he'd done to your sister might go public, and so he was able to find a way through the law, but I would always ask you what happened, did anything happen, is everything okay, and I think that one time that he kicked you in your grandmother's house, because you didn't want to pray the rosary or something like that, you were already fourteen, that's when you told me I don't want to go with that man anymore, Mom, and he became furious, I am sorry, I said, if you mistreat him I don't have to support you taking him with you, the day he wants to go with you, he can go if he wants, and so there was a time when you didn't want to see your father because things like this had happened.

WHEN ESTELA CALLED ANTONIO

As if someone had switched on a television, Antonio's sister
says, and now I know no one will be switching it off if you enter
a subway train, Antonio's sister says, the doctor says there's a
high probability you will encounter other people who are also
sick due to their minds now I know I am not a strange insect,
Antonio's sister says, I am one of those people in the train I am
worried my Mom won't accept that I am permanently sick, Antonio's sister says, but I am permanently sick, the volume of the
television just increases or decreases, how is the volume today,
Antonio says, a murmur because I am resting and sleeping a
lot, Antonio's sister says, but when I was isolated in prison I
hallucinated, Antonio's sister says, I would see Ida in a bodysuit
like a skater in a circus with a zipper for easy access down there
I couldn't differentiate between what was real and not real, Antonio's sister says, I could see you and me on the patio of our
house in Mirandela chasing our dog Pelusa and calling after her
little piggy, little piggy, and here both Antonio and his sister
laugh, because in Spanish the word for little piggy, chanchito, is
a funny word for adults to say, have they been giving you med-
icine, Antonio says, an injection once a week they're calling us
for snacks I have to go, Antonio's sister says, and so the first call
with his sister after more than a year of not hearing from her
ends and Antonio sits inside his car outside the apartment
where his daughters live, unable to type notes about her call on
his phone even though he knows the erasers in his mind are
already at work—when I was eight or nine I was babysitting our
cousin Jorge and I rubbed myself against him I think inappropriately I told the doctor already I just needed to confess that,

Antonio's sister said—don't worry too much about that you were a child, Antonio said—please don't pull an involuntary confinement on me again, Antonio's sister said—no Estelita never again you sound so well it's so good to hear from you, Antonio said, adopting the soft voice he reserves for his daughters—see? not so hard to be Nicola—yes it is—and a few days later his sister calls again but he misses her call because he's set his phone to silent as a precaution against calls or text messages from potential arrangements from Your Sugar Arrangements, but fortunately she calls again and says please never pull an involuntary confinement on me again, you can't imagine what it was like to be paranoid to begin with and then have the police come to my house, look inside my windows, and arrest me yet again without knowing why, we were worried about you, Antonio says, I interpreted it as an abuse, Antonio's sister says, so I started hallucinating that you had abused me too, you were incoherent and we were worried that something worse could happen to you, Antonio says, don't ever use that word again, Antonio's sister says, don't ever tell me I was incoherent because it's not like I've forgotten, it's not like I was sick and now that I am less sick I don't remember the times when I was sick, I know I was sick but I was happy, Antonio's sister says, I was content, please promise me you won't do it again, I won't do it again, Antonio says, promising and repromising, on their weekly calls, that he will never again set in motion an involuntary inpatient treatment against her, weekly calls, incidentally, that he receives during the weekend, so as to not interfere with his database analyst job at Prudential Investments, although he never tells her please don't call me during the workweek, no, he's not that heartless (or he is but he has learned to modulate the outward evidence of his heartlessness like everyone else), he just hasn't been able to pick up the phone whenever she calls due to conference calls,

deadlines, meetings with marketing—you did cue your sister to
avoid calling you during your workweek by saying let's talk next
Saturday or Sunday, Estelita—I don't recall I'm sorry—and so he
receives her calls once a week during weekends—what a nice
brother you have, Estela—and yet as Antonio remembers his recordings of his mother—but Mama my brother's so little—as he
imagines injecting himself with a potion that will drive him to be
like his former wife, who talks to her sister every day for as long
as he has known her, as his mother's voice inside his oversized
circumaural Sennheiser headphones courses through his body,
intermixing with the memory of his mother's voice when he was
a child, a memory that was erased long ago but that he likes to
believe could be retrieved if one day he chances upon the right
circumstances, as he stretches his banged-up body on the carpet
after catapulting himself against everyone during soccer, as he
discovers his former wife has been talking to his mother almost
every day since his sister escaped her trial proceedings—your
mother needs to talk to someone, Antonio, his former wife
said—he crosses the subspace corridor that leads to that alternative world where he hasn't spent thirty-plus years trying to
abrade his linkage to his sister and there he concludes that, although a call during the workweek would definitely interfere
with his ability to perform his database analyst job at Prudential Investments—who cares about your stupid database job
you imbecile—his sister needs him, and yes, his sister has
needed him many times before, but if years from now he were
to examine a chart of his life (with time on the X axis and crucial moments on the Y axis), he would see a significant spike in
the chart now—how easy it is to miss these crucial moments,
Antonio writes—what would be the consequences of limiting
your contact with your sister to once a week?—she might feel
that she has no support, that no one cares about her, that she's

better off dead—your sister told me she used to punch herself in the face when she was in jail, Antonio's mother said—and so he tells his sister let's talk every day, Estelita, I will block my calendar at work every day for half an hour, okay, she says, and so in between meetings about hidden Markov models and k-means clustering, he receives calls from his sister, calls that connect a Prudential Investments building in downtown Los Angeles with the mental health wing of the Spring Grove State Hospital in Catonsville, Maryland, where Antonio can hear screams in the background every time his sister calls, screams Antonio's mind tries to erase instantly, just as his mind has tried to erase the Spring Grove State Hospital in Catonsville, Maryland, where, per order of the court, Antonio's sister has to stay for a minimum of ninety days or until she regains sufficient aspects of her reason, I'm a vegetal, Antonio's sister says, I walk and sleep, walk and sleep and rehearse what I will say on my trial, don't worry we're not going to trial, Antonio says, although every time he tries to assuage her worries about a trial or about being deported (his sister neglected to apply for citizenship and her status as a permanent legal resident alien could be compromised if her charges were categorized as crimes of moral turpitude) he has to caveat his statements by saying I know it's easy for me to say, from over here, that you shouldn't worry, and I want you to know I am not trying to dismiss your concerns, which are legitimate, but based on my conversations with your lawyer, who has done a terrific job and believes we can obtain a dismissal, I don't think you have to worry about a trial, nevertheless his sister imagines and reimagines the night she was arrested in preparation for her interrogation at her trial, maybe I did have a knife, Antonio's sister says, but how did those people know I had a knife in my pocket—I can see my sister in that hospital bed, Antonio writes, facing a blank wall and talking to herself like Giorgia does when Nicola Carati's brother visits her at her mental institute—and in those rare moments on the phone when his sister asks him how he's doing he hesitates, doesn't know what to say, so instead of saying, for instance, recently I traded my old car out of despair at what's happening to you—who knows what miseries await us let's at least drive a nice car for a few years—after my sister called me I sat inside my new red German so-called luxury SUV outside the apartment where my daughters live, Antonio writes, thinking of Hershleder in The Revisionist, who sits on the doorstep of his house that is no longer his house—and instead of saying to her, for instance, that at last he'd completed his first novel and it was coming out in September—why bring up reminders of our different fates?—I can hear it in your voice, bobito—twelve years writing about Bogotá—do you remember me in those years?—of course I do—liar—he tells her about Perrito, the new family dog, about how he'd told his former wife he didn't want a dog because what difference would a dog make in their lives, about how one Saturday his former wife said let's just visit this pet supply store in Santa Monica since one of the animal shelters is having an open house there, and his former wife tricked him by saying why don't you pick our dog, you know the girls really want a dog, no, I won't, he said, but he approached the handful of dogs behind a makeshift fence on the sidewalk anyway, ven perrito, he said to one of them, adopting his dead grandmother's voice—Martina didn't talk about her upbringing but she did talk to street dogs—water for dogs / here the water for dogs—and Dora's dog walked over to him and licked his hand, and because Dora's dog looked so forlorn, and because Dora's dog wasn't Dora's dog but looked so much like Dora's dog, he said fine, this is our dog, and so Dora's dog became their dog, and after a week of arguments and counterarguments about potential names (Pongo, Fifi,

Gmail, Perrito), they agreed on Perrito, which was a fantastic name because every time anyone asks his former wife what's her dog's name she has to say, in her Czech accent, Perito — Burrito? — Perito — and when he would return home from his database analyst job at Prudential Investments, Perrito would run to greet him and pee out of excitement, and so for a while I had to pretend Perrito wasn't there so he wouldn't pee, Antonio says, and we couldn't take him on walks because he was afraid of shadows, plants, men, but he's better now, Antonio says, now he sleeps under the covers with us and prances everywhere, and so Perrito became a safe topic for them on their daily calls, how is Perrito today, Antonio's sister says, oh Perrito is sunbathing by the window, Antonio says, oh Perrito is hiding in Eva's bed, and one day he receives a card in the mail from his sister, a card printed on thin white copy paper with two rabbits on it thanking him for everything, a card he displays in the living room as a reminder that alternative worlds are possible, why weren't you like this with me before, Antonio's sister says, you used to behave as if I didn't exist, Antonio's sister says, I used to dream of going to Los Angeles to live with you, and of course Antonio doesn't have an answer for her, all he can do is say, in the softest voice he can muster, ay Estelita, and afterward hide in a conference room and cry and cry.

ANTONIO'S FORMER WIFE BY NICOLA CARATI

I would always follow her, Antonio's former wife says, my grandmother called me her tail because I would shadow her everywhere, to the point, I remember, she wanted to use the bathroom, but of course I was there, right behind her, okay can I please use the bathroom by myself, she would say, oh, okay, I'm going to wait right here, I would say, whatever she was doing I would follow her, and she would constantly tell me what she was doing, explaining it to me, okay I am spreading the oil in the frying pan, there's so much that I know because she would constantly tell me, like what, Antonio says, simple things, Antonio's former wife says, I am watering the plants right now, she would say, come Ida let's water the plants, I was her assistant, her tail assistant, her shadow, I remember walking behind her, and she would say let's water the plants, how old were you, Antonio says, it went on all my life, Antonio's former wife says, until I was ten when her Alzheimer's started and I'd reached an age when I needed to be away from everyone, and as Antonio reads the words he has transcribed from his 58:44 recording of his former wife, he tries to remember if his former wife ever followed him around as she'd done with her grandmother, not because he wants to fabricate some temporal linkage of great significance between her grandmother and him, no, of course our games from childhood live on, of course our adulthood consists of reenactments, but he, well, he doesn't know why he's trying to remember if his former wife has ever followed him around, perhaps he wants to retrofit her grandmother into his life with his former wife and his two daughters so as to feel more protected—your grandmother is still among us—of course she's still among us I think about her every day, Antonio—just as, when he was a child, he would feel more protected during his imaginary conversations with the Virgin Mary—dear mother of god today I didn't have one bad thought—think of me always—I don't talk about you anymore how could I explain you to others please forgive me—and although he can't remember one specific moment when his former wife followed him around, one of their domestic skits does include her shadowing him from room to room in silence, without touching him, pretending to have a crucial message that she's unable to verbalize along his trajectory inside their apartment, a trajectory he would prolong for her sake by inventing a menial task in the kitchen or the closet, was there something in particular that was your favorite thing to do with your grandmother, Antonio says, just be with her, Antonio's former wife says, watch the news, a soap opera that she would always watch with an apple in her hand, and I would bring my little chair and sit with her, and she would peel the apple and tell me that most of the vitamins were in the peel, there was this couple, she would say, man and woman, and the man would always peel the apple, and his wife would always bicker with him and say but all the vitamins are in the peel you shouldn't peel it, and one day the husband peeled his apple, sliced it for himself, and handed back the peel to his wife and said here's your vitamins, eat them, yes, I liked hearing that story, Antonio's former wife says, but of course Antonio would prolong his trajectory inside their apartment not only for her sake but for his, too, a trajectory that, even after she's gone (and here Antonio's surprised at how easily he can imagine his former wife at their doorstep, the day after their daughters leave them for college, a quaint suitcase on each side, her task done, ready to fly back to Czechia (when did their roles shift? because for years he was the one on their doorstep, ready to flee to

New York or Berlin or Barcelona after their daughters leave), and it occurs to Antonio that perhaps he has borrowed the image of the doorstep and the quaint suitcases from The Sound of Music or Mary Poppins, movies he'd watched for the first time at the Nuart Theatre with his daughters, both movies screened as singalongs that included a party kit (crown, glowsticks, bubbles) and two hostesses who instructed the audience on how to use the party kit and what to holler when—the curtains, Maria, the curtains!—and if years from now someone were to ask him was there something in particular that was your favorite thing to do with your daughters, he would omit any preambles about the blanks in his childhood and say the singalongs, Maria, the whole theater singing along to songs that he likes to believe he probably heard as a child but has forgotten, his daughters amazed that they're allowed to blow bubbles inside the theater, the whole theater a gyration of glowsticks during the underwater songs of The Little Mermaid (and here Antonio closes his eyes and sees the dark theater lit with glowsticks, sees a dark dance club called Universe in Chapel Hill, North Carolina, a college town where he lived with his grandparents when he was eighteen, soon after arriving to the United States (and here Antonio pauses Górecki's Miserere, removes his oversized circumaural Sennheiser headphones, and searches online for the music he'd heard at Universe twenty-two years ago—I've come down from the violet skies to save the day, a solemn trance music voice says, I'm about to reveal the tales of your life—the three-story brick building that was Universe suddenly switching from white lasers and bass to darkness and silence, except for the distant sound of spaceships, yes, he will keep his eyes closed in his cubicle and stand in the dark at Universe, marveling at a family life that shouldn't have happened to him but did, his new family next to him at the Nuart Theatre, singing their songs of the sea)), his daughters hollering the curtains, Maria, the curtains, Ada dressed as the curtains the second time they attended The Sound of Music singalong, and as he thinks of those singalongs he remembers a story about a father crying due to his son leaving for college, and although he doesn't remember many particulars of that story, he remembers wondering what kind of life do you have to live to have a father who cries when you are leaving for college (later that night, after Ada leaves them for her first sleepover, Antonio and his former wife watch old videos of Ada as a baby and he tells his former wife about the father crying for his son and Antonio cries, too, and yet the next morning he considers his reaction to that story and remembers that when he left Bogotá to attend college in the United States, his mother did cry for him—the light left the house after you left, Antonio—and so perhaps the right formulation isn't what kind of life do you have to live to have a parent who cries when you are leaving for college but what kind of upbringing do you have to procure for your children so that they're moved by your tears), a father that says, as he hopes he can say to his daughters, I was lucky to have spent all these years with you—where was I?—ah, yes, but of course I would prolong my trajectory inside our apartment not only for Ida's sake but for mine, too, a trajectory that, even after she's gone—) will continue with her at his side, shadowing him along with Dora, Silvina, his mother, la Madre Dolorosa, his sister, Ida's grandmother, shadowing him and saying, as Ida would say toward the end of their domestic skit, you don't love me anymore.

—

My grandmother was a hamster, Antonio's former wife says, a carryover after the war, I suppose, because back then you never knew what you were going to need so you had to collect everything, to the point that she would buy margarine, keep the container, wash it, and store it in her maze of a basement, where you could find these humongous old wooden closets from before World War II, which contained her dresses, little pieces of jewelry, buttons, sewing equipment, I could open a drawer and spend hours looking at these little treasures, do you remember some of them, Antonio says, I remember my grandmother's feather coats, Antonio's former wife says, my Mom told me my grandmother was always beautifully dressed, and her makeup was perfect, her jewelry matching, no jeans or pants, because women didn't wear jeans or pants, but I don't remember her this way because as a kid that wasn't what mattered to me, how I remember her is in her favorite dress, which unfortunately was plastic, with a lot of static, which she would wear every day, how do you mean plastic, Antonio says, acrylic, Antonio's former wife says, gray and green with little flowers, an acrylic dress that would sparkle with static against her tights when she would undress, and so my Mom also told me that when my grandmother was younger she would change three times a day, and she would ride a scooter to town, whereas when I remember her she didn't ride anymore because she had eighty-six breaks in her bones, she was limping in one leg, her knee couldn't fold, so she would just live in her kitchen, her bedroom, she had a little garden on the side of the house gated from the dogs, her kingdom, her garden, her world, she built her little world in our house and didn't leave it, so she didn't talk about the outside world, the way she remembered it, was she part of the resistance during the war, Antonio says, I think she was somehow involved with the antipropaganda newspaper, Antonio's former wife says, and here Antonio pauses his 58:44 recording of his former wife and remembers the massive World War II history book he'd read on his first trip to Český Krumlov, almost twelve years ago, back when he was still trying to avoid traveling to far away countries because he didn't want to disrupt the world he was trying to build inside his first novel, a world populated with his memories of Bogotá, him playing soccer at his Jesuit high school, for instance, him conducting imaginary conversations with the Virgin Mary, a world so tenuous, so pockmarked already that a long trip to Czechia might relegate some of his memories to the dark corners of a place like the Central Registry in All the Names by José Saramago, where the index cards for the dead are stored, him on a plane to Czechia reading about the impact of the war on Czechia and Poland, and although he doesn't remember any of its contents, he does remember feeling like he was carrying a portable coffin due to its thickness, its black cover, its cast of doomed resistance fighters, so that, by the time his plane landed, the Czechia of his former wife had become the Czechia invaded by the Germans, who had orders to exterminate buildings and people, although over the years the Czechia of the war also became the Czechia of his former wife's parents, who, on his first trip to Czechia, tested Antonio's endurance to Chopin, their favorite vodka: on Monday the mother would serve Antonio Chopin shots and the father would complain about her serving herself too many Chopin shots, leaving the table in a huff, on Tuesday the father would serve Antonio Chopin shots and the mother would complain about him serving himself too many Chopin shots, leaving the table in a huff, yes, Antonio thinks, he'd enjoyed their brand of bantering (neither of his former wife's parents spoke English or Spanish so he'd interpreted their exchange as bantering), and after his former wife's parents became resigned to him being the father of their two granddaughters, they welcomed him into their family, and although he detested the exhaustion that stayed with him for weeks after flying to Czechia, he'd flown there multiple times, toward the end of summer #1, for instance, six months after Ada was born, soon after

he'd called his former wife in Český Krumlov and told her he
didn't know how long he could continue to playact at being father and husband.

—

My grandmother on my father's side was murdered, Antonio's
former wife says, two weeks before my aunt's wedding, while
everyone was preparing for it, back then it wasn't like you just
drove to the store, you had to grow your own pig, make your
own sausages, so they were storing everything in the barn, and
my grandmother happened to need something from the barn,
where someone had been hiding, and this someone smashed
her head with an ax and killed her, and so my dad, since he was
the oldest, had to be involved in the investigation, and when
your mother did her work on my dad, when they were both
staying with us, my dad opened up, and it was scary because my
dad doesn't talk, especially not about his Mom, he just started
talking and talking and couldn't stop, what work did my Mom
do on your dad, Antonio says, your Mom did Reiki on him, Antonio's former wife says, your Mom's theory about my dad going
blind is that he doesn't want to see, which is weird because if
you think about my dad, he's incredibly intuitive, really good
with people, but as far as emotions, he pretends they don't exist,
so many things he pretends they don't exist, kind of like you,
I didn't even know about the head thing, so your Mom didn't
know how it was going to turn out when she was holding her
hands above my dad's head, she said she feels this heavy weight
above him, and she sees his Mom, only the head, everything
else is dark, as if the rest of her body didn't exist, no eyes, just
the head, and she said she sees my dad not wanting to see, and
I was translating her words to my dad, and of course he was
trying to be silly about it, but afterward his face changed and
later he told me that, after his mother's funeral, after she was

buried and everything, the investigation had gone on and on, and the police were so pissed they couldn't find the murderer that they decided to dig up her grave, and my dad had to identify her, and they didn't want to dig everything out so they just chopped off the head, and my dad had to identify his own mother, which you can imagine after six months it's not just bone it's still flesh, swollen, smells, it's partially eaten by bugs, worms are sticking out, and he had to identify his own mother this way, and he did and then passed out, so when I was telling your Mom about my dad losing his eyesight, she said it's all linked to his inability to, I didn't even remember his mother existed, Antonio, I always thought everyone has only one grandmother, I didn't know she even existed because my father never mentioned her — whenever I think about my former wife's father, Antonio writes, I think about Ida flying to Czechia for three days to surprise her father for his seventieth birthday, or I think about Ida during summer #6, driving to the hospital in Prague every day to sit by him while the surgeons decided what to do about his ailing heart — what do you remember most about those days when your father was in the hospital, Antonio said, the traffic, Antonio's former wife said, the traffic because from our house in Český Krumlov to the hospital in Prague I had to drive for two hours, and sometimes I would roll up the windows, turn up the radio, and scream, just as I used to do as a teenager, when my Mom would shut the windows of our house, turn up the music, and tell us to scream or bark or growl, what else do you remember about those trips to the hospital, Antonio said, the phones always ringing at the nurses' station, the sounds of those ancient, stationary phones, now whenever my dad and I hear those phones anywhere we shudder — so you know all this pretending his mother's murder didn't happen, Antonio's former wife says, pretending his mother didn't exist,

grieving after the funeral but never again after that, because according to my mother my father and his two brothers met at our
house after the funeral and locked themselves in the bedroom
for three days, drinking nonstop, and my uncle's wife and my
Mom would prepare food, knock on the door, deliver the food
and leave, and they would keep drinking, but after that, after
those three days, they left the house and didn't grieve again,
goodbye, like nothing ever happened, never any pictures of her,
nothing, gone, puff.

—

My childhood was a blast, Antonio's former wife says, I grew
up surrounded by greenhouses, a walnut tree forest, and so
much land that I could vanish and no one would even notice,
or I could build my own bonfires and no one would tell me
oh you're going to burn yourself, or I could hide behind the
trees, or I could venture out to our three detached garages, by
my dad's workstation, that was another activity of mine back
then, watching my dad fixing things, I think that's why I'm so
good at it too, I would spend hours next to my dad watching
him fixing and building, and every weekend, since there was
nothing else to do, my parents and their friends would meet in
someone's house and throw a party, and there would be music,
dancing, tons of alcohol, Coca Cola from the black market, and
the kids would just roam around the farm, because all of our
friends were farmers, what else do you remember about your
parents when you were growing up, Antonio says, they didn't
worry, Antonio's former wife says, no one checked where I was,
they were always busy and they partied a lot, every weekend they
would either take us with them or they would leave us with our
grandmother, and if they went by themselves they would come
back with more guests and would continue the party at our
house, what about your Mom, Antonio says, my Mom was the

one who played with us because my dad had to wake up at three in the morning or he was on the farm, Antonio's former wife says, he did take us ice-skating though, but my Mom was the one who would always pick up some kids from the other farmers and take us sledding, or hiking, or to the pool, kind of like I do, funny, what else do you remember about your dad, Antonio says, the greenhouses were our primary income, Antonio's former wife says, and there was this plan that consisted of my dad bringing aszparagus seeds from the United States, asparagus, Antonio says, no asparagus is food here, Antonio's former wife says, anyway you added aszparagus to bouquets of flowers, and because back then there was nothing in the stores, and in Czechia, in Czech culture, if you visit someone's house you don't arrive empty-handed, you always bring something, and since there was nothing else in the stores, you would always arrive with a bouquet of flowers, so every morning, at three in the morning, my dad would load these bunches of green thingies, these aszparagus thingies, drive to the bazaar and sell them there, and he would make a lot of money from it, so he would come back home, back then we had no banks, no credit cards, so it was all cash operated, so he would always come home with stacks of money, and my dad would count the money as fast as a machine, always, every morning, by the time he was back at seven from the bazaar, I would be getting ready for school and I would see him at the table counting the money, it was amazing, he can still count as fast as a machine, although no one has that much cash anymore, did your parents ever hit you, Antonio says, never, Antonio's former wife says, my dad I think I remember once when I was maybe six or seven, we were going to a dance class and my Mom drove us there and left us while she went downstairs to the store, hoping they would have something, and we saw that the class was canceled so we went back down to the store but couldn't find her, the car was still outside so we went back inside, but in the meantime she'd left the store and we see her driving away so we run toward the car, it's like fifteen minutes from our house walking, so it wasn't far but it was already 7:00 p.m., but because I was little I couldn't make it, of course the car is faster, and my sister is superfast, and I keep running and running but I can't make it, so I start walking, and my sister leaves me there and runs home, and when I arrive home she tells my parents that I saw friends and left with them somewhere, and because my parents were so worried about me, my dad hit me with a belt I think, I don't remember, I was so confused, you left me there and I am getting hit, so that was the only time my dad hit me, but I know he was just so scared that something had happened to me.

—

My sister was a difficult child, Antonio's former wife says, she didn't sleep, was colicky, cranky, would always cry, the entire house would take turns staying up with her because she only slept during the day, or she only slept if someone rocked her stroller, and when she was two years old Ida was born, and Ida was perfect, Ida didn't cry, Ida was always smiling, slept through the night, and everyone started falling in love with Ida, so suddenly all this attention my sister had for two years went away because everyone was fascinated by how good Ida was and how bad she was, and look how good Ida is and you are such a bad girl, and of course now everyone knows what a mistake it is to say that, but given her personality, her temper, that was just the worst you could do as far as siblings, and I still remember how they would say oh look Ida is eating everything, because if you gave me pork I would eat pork, if you gave me an apple I would eat the apple, I was fat and chubby and I was cheerful and I had red cheeks and I was healthy and she was sickly and skinny and little and she only wanted to eat hard-boiled eggs, so what would she do to you, Antonio says, she would just create situations to get me in trouble, and she would use how naïve I was and my need to be loved by her, accepted by her, because I was so naïve, I wasn't a clever child, I wasn't sneaky, she would use that to manipulate me, for instance she would play cards with me and she would cheat, so I would constantly lose, and she would set up the game so that the loser would have to do chores, for instance we had a sofa bed and every morning we had to take our sheets and fold them, and in the evening we had to spread out the sheets and the blankets again, and the loser had to do it for the other person, and of course if she was cheating, I was so stupid and naïve, she would always win, oh and if you didn't do it by seven you had to do it an extra ten times, so I would have to make her bed a hundred and fifty times, and if I didn't do it she would hit me, or she would break my toys, and her being angry at me was so scary, I hated that feeling, when she was in a weird mood, angry or mad, she would take it out on me the most, or little things like she would lock me in that sofa bed, but I hear that is very common, she would drag me in there by my hair and lock me there, and because our house was so big, even if my parents wanted to intervene, my Mom was either in the kitchen, or cleaning, or doing laundry, we are on a farm, my dad is out working, there's no way anyone would see it happening, unlike in an apartment where it's so easy, you turn around, you see it, you hear it, no one would hear me in this humongous house, and by the time she would let me out we both would rush to my Mom and I would say Mom she locked me in the bed and she would say what, I would never do such a thing, and so who do you believe, I can't blame my parents for not seeing it, my Mom when I asked her about it she said when we would fight and she couldn't take it anymore she would take me to my grandmother and my sister to my grandfather, who was an alcoholic, and she would make drinks for him, light cigarettes for him, he had a bunch of multivitamins, which were very sweet, and she would eat them, hey, we survived, but the scariest incident was when my parents were changing the heating for the greenhouses from coal to gas, and for that they needed a different furnace, so my dad ordered this huge furnace, steel, with a bunch of doors and pipes inside, and it wasn't hooked up yet, it was still standing inside our garage, and there was a party in our house, of course, and the kids were running and playing hide-and-seek, and my sister talked me into going into that furnace and she locked me in there and left, I don't know how long it lasted, it was pretty long because when I came out everyone was leaving, again, huge farm, no supervision, no way anyone could hear me, I could have easily died, there wasn't enough oxygen, but there were these layers of pipes, so I squeezed myself in and around the pipes, up and up, and there was a tiny little window to look inside and see if the furnace was burning properly, and that wasn't latched so I pushed it open and somehow pushed myself through and came out, and instead of going to my parents and saying you know what your goddamned daughter did, I went to my sister and said na na fu fu, look, I escaped.

—

Sometimes after arriving home from his eight hours of SQL queries at Prudential Investments, Antonio lingers on the stairs by the doorstep, unzipping the boots of his work costume and listening to the children's music inside, the lyrics in Czech, of course, a language that, despite reminding him of the garbled, invented language in The Silence by Ingmar Bergman (the white noise of Bergman's train the same as that of the airplanes on his way to Czechia), soothes him, and as he unzips his reasonable work boots—so friends, Wendell Berry says, every day do something that won't compute—his database analyst boots that do compute—there's man all over for you, Didi says, blaming on his boots the faults of his feet—twice a week I bandage my feet before playing soccer, Antonio thinks, and twice a week I limp to work because my left foot hasn't recovered from its previous injury—he considers how his attempts to deplete his body through soccer have allowed him to momentarily rest from his linkage with his sister, as if by draining the batteries of the antenna in charge of receiving signals from his sister he can be momentarily at peace, and perhaps the Czech language, which although familiar still doesn't compute for him—Czech sounds like Russian to me, Antonio thinks, and when I think of Czech I think of the poems in The Mirror by Tarkovsky's father—no more dinner for you if you compare Czech with Russian ever again, his former wife said—has contributed to his recurring disbelief that he still shares this warm apartment with his former wife and his two daughters, although if he had to explain his current living arrangement he would have to diagram a timeline whereas he lived at Home with his former wife and his two daughters (t1), The Other Home next door to Home but visited every day after work plus Saturday (t2), The Other Home next door to Home but was allowed to sleep at Home three days a week (t3), and in that interval between (t1) and (t2) he might pause and explain that in the aftermath of their divorce proceedings his visits to Home consisted mostly of him taking Ada to the pool at the Jewish Community Center, the only location nearby where they could spend time together in the evening during the workweek without his former wife, the reverberations inside the underground pool facility like those inside a cathedral or a submarine, the occasional Russian

grandfathers wading into the adult pool, their bellies like float-
ers, the kids' pool empty, the warm water to his chest when he
sat with his legs outstretched, an awkward sitting position, like
someone's wry idea of levitation, alternating between a feeling
of vacancy and an overwhelming desire to produce warm father and daughter memories for Ada, as he'd tried to do in a
one-page memoir piece entitled Fathers Fated, which he'd ad-
dressed to Ada and had set during the first time they attend a
performance of The Velveteen Rabbit — a father in the audience
was crying, Antonio wrote, you didn't notice because you were
pointing at the crocodile on the stage — a piece he'd never tried
to publish because he'd been unable to capture both the wonder of the moment — you placed your finger to your lips as a
reminder of the silence we'd agreed on, Antonio wrote, twirled
your hands above your head like we'd practiced after your ballet
class, shuffled in your seat because you were so little that the
seat would fold in on you if you didn't sit on the edge — and
the disbelief he felt at being a new father — before the show
you ran in the garden outside as if you'd just snatched the
ball from the dachshund you'd been petting, Antonio wrote,
the patter of your slippers on the grass reminded me of nothing and that was wonderful — Ada splashing the surface of the
kids' pool inside a cathedral or a submarine and him splashing after her as Tata Shark — everywhere we went I saw grandmothers looking at us and marveling at a world where fathers
and daughters held hands, Antonio wrote — wonder and disbelief but also an impulse to record their time together — soon
after our first Velveteen Rabbit I purchased my first camera,
Antonio wrote, I needed the evidence that it was possible, that
that father was really me — and yet the videos are also for you,
Antonio wrote, I like to believe that if you ever decide not to see
me again, like my sister and I did with my father years before

you were born, you can watch how we were together and change
your mind—and after their pool sessions Antonio would cross
the dark laundry room between Home and The Other Home
(Antonio abhors overt symbolism in his own so-called fictions,
plus the outside world barely exists for him in retrospect so he
can't concoct symbols out of blank landscapes, but because he
has been crossing this laundry room for so many years, and
because the laundry room looks like a dilapidated basement
with cables like entrails, storage spaces like coffins, rats like eels
either slithering by or trying to wriggle free from their traps,
television voices coming from the ceiling threatening one another in a language that doesn't compute for Antonio, an old
tenant with a disfigured mouth who wears a homemade plastic raincoat and patrols her washing machine, he has come to
associate the laundry room with purgatory), returning to The
Other Home, also known as his quaint nook, where he would
panfry his meat and tortilla dinner while listening to Michael
Silverblatt saying to a group of Oulipo members that as a child
he loved math—dear Mr. Silverblatt, Antonio writes, during a
rough interval in my life, when I couldn't read or write in the
aftermath of my divorce proceedings, I found consolation in
the sound of your voice—dear Mr. Silverblatt I wanted your
voice to be a father asking me about fractals—yes, sometimes
when he enters the apartment where his daughters live he still
feels like an intruder, or like a prospective renter being shown
an apartment that comes with furniture and a family, or like a
character in one of those Christmas movies who is given the
chance to watch how his life might have turned out if he hadn't,
for instance, abandoned his children as Antonio had planned to
do after his second daughter was born, not abandon them, no,
leave them in their mother's custody so as to become a weekend
visitor, but most of the time he can't linger on his doorstep for

too long because his daughters know the sound of his motorcycle so by the time he climbs the stairs the door is already opened and Ada is saying Tata come see my new storybook, and Eva is saying hurry come see the platypus I drew for you, and their new dog Perrito is jumping and peeing out of excitement, and his former wife is preparing dinner for this family of his, which, amazingly, still includes him.

S 9

WHEN ANTONIO WAS ANTONIO

One of the secretaries at Mitsubishi called me and said your father was involved with his eighteen-year-old secretary, Antonio's mother says, and that she wanted me to know because he could lose his job because of this dalliance, and since this girl was from Barranquilla, that year he wanted to spend his birthday in Barranquilla, but his plan was to leave us at his aunt's house in Barranquilla and for him to stay at a hotel, and so I said no, I'm not going, if you want to see your secretary I don't have a problem with you driving there by yourself, leave me in peace with my children, moreover, I am going to the beach with your parents, no, he said, you're going to do what I say, and that's when he slapped me, so this is when it happened, Antonio says, because Antonio had heard about this incident years ago but hadn't heard about the secretary from Barranquilla, although he's heard of the other women near the house in Mirandela, whom his father would visit in the evenings, whenever he said he was going for a walk and a smoke around the block (and here Antonio declines to link his father's extramarital activities to his own YSA activities because what would be the point of that? to say to himself see, you can't escape that individual? — I might have contemplated leaving Ida when Eva was born, just as that individual contemplated leaving my mother when I was born, Antonio writes, but I have never contemplated doing what that individual did to my sister and his stepdaughter—), yes, Antonio's mother says, because I didn't obey him, and so I defended myself, and the neighbor started shouting if I hear you're doing anything to your wife my sons and I are coming for you and we're armed, and that's when I called your uncle Lucho,

and Lucho said I am coming there now, I'm getting that son of a
bitch out of there with bullets, and you can't stay there, you have
to leave that house because you've endured too much abuse, and
so collect the clothes you need for the kids, whatever you feel you
need, and you leave that place, so when I told your father Lucho
was coming, armed, he disappeared, that's how I was able to take
you out and escape from that house, well, Estela wasn't there
because she was spending the long weekend in Cartagena with
my friend Blanca, so you were there by yourself, and perhaps because Antonio knows what his mother is about to say in this part
of the recording, he notices her long, dispirited sigh, knowing,
on the one hand, that as a mother she shouldn't display her help-
lessness in front of her child (because if a mother can't pretend
life is worth living . . .), and on the other hand what his mother
is about to say already happened, it's irreversible, and that was
tough on you, Antonio's mother says, because at first, after hearing his shouting, you hid, but all of a sudden you were there, between me and your father, shouting to your father don't treat my
mother like that, and that's when your father hit you — my father
swats me away and my brain activates its emergency erasure
mechanisms, Antonio writes, erasing that moment and, just in
case, everything that came before it — and I said to your father
I told you the day you touch me or the children all of this ends,
you're never leaving this house, he shouted, and since the neighbor started shouting as well, because remember the house didn't
have glass windows, only wire mesh so the neighbors could hear
everything, and I called Lucho and your father heard what I'd
said to him, and so after your father was gone and I was able to
leave our bedroom where he'd cornered me, I went looking for
you and I found you under your bed, trembling, and here Antonio pauses the recording and closes his eyes, trying to remember that moment — and when I am old and alone and banished

from my loved ones, Antonio writes, I will retrieve that bed from storage and wait for the end underneath it — no, he can't remember that moment, although he does remember having nightmares in that bed and his mother coming to assuage him at night, remembers the purple dinosaur that he would clutch in that bed, the Elmo he was scared of, I went looking for you and I found you under your bed, Antonio's mother says, trembling, and I said no, I have not been thinking about you, I've only been thinking about myself, I've been a coward, so I picked you up, picked up some clothes, and I said we are leaving, no more, this will never happen again.

WHEN ARTURO WAS BILL VIOLA

I prosecuted my father, Daria said, although my mother didn't want to press charges so I had to provide my statement alone and attend his trial alone, how old were you, Antonio said, thirteen, Daria said, just seeing my father in dreams terrifies me, Antonio said, although I'm used to these apparitions by now and they don't happen too often, I see my father in my dreams too, Daria said, but I'm most terrified to run into him in this reality so I've told my friends that if I ever ask them for a quick exit they should take me seriously—dear Daria, Antonio writes, you're the most courageous woman I've ever met—I remember waking up late at night and seeing my mother in our living room, Karla said, staring out the window in the dark, like an automaton programmed to power off at night because her owner was asleep and no household chores were needed, and so in honor of this memory of her, Karla said, one of my earliest memories of my mother, Arturo, because my mother is the subject of most of my performances, I reenacted the punishment my mother knew from school in Seoul at a busy street corner of Koreatown in Los Angeles, a punishment that consisted of tilting her body forward and keeping her arms raised (and here Antonio searches online for corporal punishment + Korea + school and finds too many variations on her mother's punishment)—on my father's birthday my mother asked me and my sister to tell Dad that we wanted to leave Tokyo and return to the United States, Hannah said, and so we told him and Dad left the dinner table and locked himself in the bathroom, why did your mother ask you to say that, Antonio said, because she wanted to return to her lover in California, Hannah said, whom she'd met at a play-

ground while Dad was finishing his graduate program—dear
Hannah, Antonio writes, I can see myself in your father, locked
in the bathroom to conceal his despair, although I like to believe if you and your sister were my daughters I wouldn't have
let you go—we had a good time but I don't want to see you
anymore, Artemisia from UCLA messages him while Antonio's
on a conference call about the geometric distributed lag marketing model he has built in between SQL queries, you treated
me well and don't take it personally but it's hurting me, I want
to have a healthy relationship not an arrangement, I see the
way waitresses look at us and I feel low, I know people are judging
our age difference and I can't handle this shame anymore—
Artemisia wanted to become an attorney, Antonio writes later
that day, so she was studying philosophy when I met her on
Your Sugar Arrangements—send me your class syllabus
please—what is the mind?—let's watch The Shining at the Nuart
Theatre and smoke some jays—goodbye, dear Artemisia—in
town for summer break can I see you tonight, Jasmine messages
him while Antonio's on a conference call trying to explain to sun-
dry marketing managers the methodology pitfalls of attitudinal
segmentation, tonight it is, Antonio replies, although after the
Goth Raver incident Antonio should be avoiding these kinds of
encounters but instead he just tries to schedule fewer of them,
wondering, each time he slips away at 9:15 p.m., whether this will
be the night that destroys his life, which of course increases the
thrill of these encounters (not only for him but for his arrangements as well since they're slipping away from their dorms or
their parents' basement (Vera, for instance, had taken him to
her mother's basement through a side door and a dark corridor
and when her mother heard them she yelled at them from above
and Vera yelled back in the same island language—Vera's basement had a sleeping bag instead of a bed, Antonio writes, but

it did have plenty of rugs, scented candles, immense canvases with hundreds of doodles on them, splotched cans of paint—)), I've finalized a plea agreement for your sister, Antonio's sister's attorney messages him, so she will be transferred from the hospital to Baltimore City jail this week, Roger Sessions's Piano Sonata No. 2, Jasmine says later that evening in answer to his question about what she has been playing, play it for me, Antonio says, because they're at the Frates Cafe, where chamber musicians can drop in to play Mozart, Beethoven, Bach, and perhaps because of Jasmine's outfit, which brings to mind a flight attendant en route to Maui (white jeans, blue blazer, handkerchief around her neck), or because of her long black hair down to her waist that Antonio knows she'll ask him to pull later—I know you know I don't need to ask you, Arturo—or because she's petite and smiles too much on her way to the upright piano, too eager to please, removing her blazer and handing it to Antonio, who bows to her, glad to add intrigue to the performance by pretending to be her servant, or because the Frates Cafe brings to mind the cafe in the movie Shine, where David Helfgott, a pianist whose formulae of reality have been distorted, sneaks in to perform Flight of the Bumblebee—I mean, the point is, David Helfgott says, if you do something wrong you can be punished for the rest of your life—the audience is taken aback by the speed of Jasmine's fingers and the severity of her sound, as is Antonio, who hasn't acknowledged just yet that for him this vision of Jasmine plus Roger Sessions equals an onrush greater than those caused by, say, pornographic videos of rural Russian women selling fruit while underneath the counter men lick their legs, and after Jasmine is done rebuking the audience that condescended to her inside this cafe that reminds Antonio of Amsterdam, even though Antonio has never been to Amster-

dam, Antonio and Jasmine drink from a pitcher of cheap sangria while occasionally a scrawny Caucasian American violist
who has no chance whatsoever with Jasmine interrupts them,
trying to impress her with his role as organizer of local concerts, you okay to drive, he says, eyeing Antonio as if suspecting
him of trying to take advantage of her excess of sangria, don't
worry he's driving, Jasmine says, and so Antonio drives her
mother's 1980s BMW to The Other Home, where he, distracted
by the intensity of his desire for her, forgets to cover her
mouth — she shrieked as I imagined an eagle would shriek, De-
nis Johnson says, and it felt wonderful to be alive to hear
it — which culminates in his neighbor banging on their shared
wall and then on his front door, and perhaps because of his disbelief that his neighbor exists (Antonio has never seen his
neighbor), or because Antonio and Jasmine are silent and still
now and isn't that the point (why is the neighbor still banging
on the door?), he takes too long to wrap himself in blankets and
open the door, it's one in the morning can you shut the hell up,
his neighbor says, okay, Antonio says, too unapologetically
(because if his neighbor would have been a man he would be
egging on Antonio instead of interrupting him, no? — dale con
todo, Bruja—), and the next morning, after opening all the windows to air out the place and showering in silence, his empty
apartment seems, as usual, unreal to him — a Japanese pianist
was here last night? and she woke you up twice in the middle of
the night because she wanted to keep going? — I don't believe it
either — and as usual, once he has purged his body of any evidence of wrongdoing, a purge that reminds him of Bill Viola's
Inverted Birth, which he watched at Disney Hall with Katerina,
also known as Uzi Kitten, he crosses the laundry room that connects his building with the building where his daughters live

(a laundry room that every week seems more populated by other people's junk (bicycles with handwritten warning signs, boxes with pictures of electric heaters)), and when his former wife opens the door Antonio immediately knows something's wrong because she doesn't greet him — good morning, Tato, she doesn't say — was there someone at your apartment last night, his former wife says, what are you talking about, Antonio says, the building manager messaged me that there was a noise complaint from your neighbor last night, his former wife says, that's strange, Antonio says, allowing her question no importance whatsoever, and while in the kitchen Antonio continues to pretend that this is all probably due to some irrelevant misunderstanding, his former wife picks up his keys, crosses the laundry room, enters his apartment, returns, and says don't ever talk to me again, walking out and driving away, and once he's sure she has gone he crosses the laundry room, enters his apartment and finds, by his bed, the dog collar he'd fastened on Jasmine's neck (how is it that he remembered to hide the metal leash that hooks to the collar and dispose of the vinyl tape he tied around Jasmine's wrists but forgot to hide the collar? — you and your stupid Bill Viola showers, Arturo—), and that day and the next everything at the apartment where his daughters live is as before except Ida pretends he doesn't exist, although every now and then she asks him a harmless logistical question so as to not alert the children about their rift, and as the days go by Antonio hopes she will resort to her own erasure mechanisms, and because she has given no indication that she's planning to resort to them he tallies what he could offer her to slowly overturn her pretending he doesn't exist, for instance moving to Czechia, or giving up The Other Home, as Ida has suggested several times through the years, although the latter offering terrifies him because The Other Home has allowed him to skirt the disastrous father / husband reimaging that had been activated when he married Ida nine years ago (if current role = husband and father, then Antonio = Antonio's father), in other words by calling Ida his former wife he isn't a husband, and by having another home he isn't a father (if current role <> father / husband, then Antonio = Nicola).

WHEN ANTONIO RECEIVED CALLS FROM
BALTIMORE CITY JAIL

The automated system informs Antonio he's receiving a call from an inmate of Baltimore City jail, an inmate called Estela Jiménez, the words Estela and Jiménez a recording of his sister saying Estela and Jiménez, the automated system informs Antonio that the call will be recorded and monitored, if you have questions or complaints about this call please call customer service, to hear the cost of this call, press 8, to accept this call, press 5, to decline this call, hang up, so Antonio presses 5 and the automated system informs him it requires a credit card to fund an account from which to deduct the cost of this call, so Antonio enters his credit card number and funds an account for $10 and the automated system informs him he has a balance of $1.35 because there's a $8.65 service charge, please hold while you are connected, the automated system disconnects the call, the automated system doesn't acknowledge its error because it doesn't register it as an error, unless the automated system contains the appropriate error-handling code, of course, an SQL syntax as basic as if account = funded and call < 0.01 seconds, then error = 1, else error = 0, the automated system doesn't tabulate how long Estela Jiménez has been holding the public phone to her ear due to the automated process of accepting a collect call from an inmate of Baltimore City jail, unless the chief executive officer of the company that owns the automated system also happens to have a sister whose impaired mind has led her to become an inmate of a county jail and therefore he, the brother, has set quarterly company goals to reduce the length of the automated process of accepting collect calls from

inmates at county jails—let us not lengthen the suffering of
those who are already suffering—the automated system doesn't
wonder what Estela Jiménez might be thinking as she waits for
its automated process to complete—has my brother tired of me
already? did he reject the call and the system hasn't registered
the rejection yet? has my brother tired of being reminded that
he's linked to my miseries?—I'm here, Estelita—the automated
system informs Antonio he's receiving a call from an inmate
of Baltimore City jail, you're receiving a call from an inmate of
Baltimore City jail, the automated system says, to accept this
call, press 5, yes, okay, Antonio presses 5, Toñio, Antonio's sister
says, I've just read in Mundo Hispánico that immigrants who
have committed a crime will be immediately deported so I've
decided not to accept the plea agreement because I don't want
to be deported, the automated system disconnects the call, the
automated system doesn't acknowledge its error because there is
no error but a depletion of the $1.35 in his account, and so out-
side of Menotti's Coffee Stop, where he likes to read on Sunday
afternoons because the sun on his face allows him to read for
hours without falling asleep, Antonio waits for the automated
system to link him to his sister again, the automated system informs Antonio he's receiving a call from an inmate of Baltimore
City jail, an inmate called Estela Jiménez, the automated system accepts the $25 from his credit card and the autorecharge
option (how many brothers and mothers and sisters, rushing
through this automated process, end up misdialing their credit
card numbers? how many fathers worry that the long wait on the
other end of the line might change their daughters irreversibly?),
the automated system informs Antonio the charges will appear
under GTL Inmate Phone Services, which he, a database analyst
for Prudential Investments, knows is the kind of data signal
a credit card company can mine by querying a transaction

statement description field, yes, a database analyst can run a simple SQL query with a like %inmate% statement in the where clause to select all records that contain the word inmate in the transaction statement description field, which might lead a database analyst to conclude that Antonio is in jail, do you have a few minutes, a database analyst might say to his database manager, I think the presence of the term %inmate% in our credit transactions might be a leading indicator that a customer won't have the money to pay us back, so I was thinking we could build a test to minimize charge-offs by significantly reducing the credit line of those customers with transactions that include %inmate%, no, a more experienced database analyst might say, the presence of %inmate% isn't enough, to verify they're in jail you will need to run another query to check whether these customers continue to transact after the word %inmate% surfaces in their transaction history, right, the junior database analyst might say, I will need to (a) check these post-%inmate% transactions are a different pattern of transactions as those before %inmate%, (b) exclude post-%inmate% transactions that could be considered recurring payments, (c) verify post-%inmate% transactions are occurring at merchants that would require his or her physical presence, exactly, the senior database analyst might say, plus what if they were in jail but they're out on bond now, we are better off just A / B testing whether %inmate% gives us any significant net reduction on charge-offs, Toñio, Antonio's sister says, I've just read in Mundo Hispánico that immigrants who have committed a crime will be immediately deported, a crime in this case includes domestic violence, DUI, petty thefts, among others, but you're pleading to three counts of public disturbance, Antonio says, which does not fall under the category of crimes of moral turpitude, the kind of crimes that will lead to deportation according to our immigration attorney, that's not what the newspaper says, Antonio's sister says, the newspaper doesn't have enough space to print all the categories of crimes that will lead to deportation, Antonio says, DUI, petty thefts, among others, Antonio's sister says, we don't know what's in the among others category, Antonio says, if they deport me will you come see me, Antonio's sister says, of course, Antonio says, how am I going to live in Bogotá, Antonio's sister says, please don't worry about that I will support you, Antonio says, but they won't deport you, Estelita, I checked with the immigration attorney, I know you're nervous, I would be too, but we're almost there, Estelita, please accept the plea, I'm sorry, Antonio's sister says, I can't do it, no.

WHEN NICOLA WAS ANTONIO

What I don't transcribe I will forget, Antonio thinks as he reviews the metadata of his recording of his mother, which he has
been jotting down on his sketchbook and which consists of
timestamps at the beginning of threads, his mother's phrases
as headlines to these threads, downward L-shaped arrows linking headlines to subheadlines, stars next to significant headlines,
checkmarks next to headlines he has already transcribed, and
although Antonio suspects that what he doesn't transcribe he
will forget, he also suspects that what he does transcribe he will
forget, too (already he has forgotten sizable portions of the Bogotá he spent twelve years writing about, for instance), so perhaps he's been transcribing his recording of his mother not to
document those horrible days of childhood so that one day he
can write about them but to spend these horrible days of adulthood in the company of her voice — I'm tired of encountering
mental institutes and lunar landscapes when I'm asleep let's
stroll to a carnival with Ada and Eva and wave at the college
students dressed like salmons, Ida — one day I will jump-start a
mother business, Antonio writes, a business that will ware-
house recordings of your mothers so when your turn for the
horrible comes you can press a button on your phone and receive not a call from your mothers (because what would you say
to them if they called?) but a call with a recording of your mothers saying that when you were little you sold water for dogs — yes,
Antonio thinks, what I don't transcribe I will forget and what I
do transcribe I will forget — nevertheless Antonio still wants to
at least try to retain these moments he hasn't transcribed — what
is to be done with moments that have no place of their own in

time, Bruno Schulz says, moments that have occurred too early
or too late, after the whole of time has been distributed?—what
is to be done about his mother saying when you were little the
three of us were like a junta, which Antonio hasn't transcribed
yet (too fragmentary), or his mother saying Estela was very pro-
tective of you, I mean, your sister started to talk when she was
eight months old, and one day, when you were still a newborn,
you peed while I was changing your diaper on the couch,
splashing me like a lawn sprinkler, and I complained and said
something like uff, this darn child, and your sister admonished
me and said but Mama, he's little, which Antonio hasn't transcribed yet (too sentimental), or his mother saying a man on the
street in downtown Bogotá approached me and said your
daughter is so beautiful, please be careful someone could steal
her, which Antonio hasn't transcribed yet (too foreboding), or
his mother saying your sister painted stories and she would ask
me to sew the pages to make them into a book just like Eva does,
which Antonio hasn't transcribed yet (too heartbreaking), or
his mother saying I kept your childhood drawings in a box, but
when we escaped from that house in Mirandela the box stayed
behind, and I did ask your father to give it back but he refused,
so unfortunately I was never able to save your drawings as
you've done, Antonio, all those drawings of Ada and Eva on
your kitchen walls, and a month after we escaped, Antonio's
mother said, thieves emptied that house in Mirandela, taking
both televisions, your father's expensive stereo, his collection of
Italian shoes, his canvases with his abstract paintings, everything
(and here Antonio can imagine Don Jorge, the old neighbor
who would hand him toffees through the wire fence, snacking
on popcorn and grinning as the thieves loaded their truck with
his father's crap), which Antonio hasn't transcribed yet (too unbelievable due to how quickly retribution came to his father),

or his mother saying every time I would tell your sister we have to talk about what's been happening with your father, she would say no, I don't want to talk about him (his father had remarried a woman who came with a fourteen-year-old daughter, and instead of taking this fourteen-year-old daughter to her confirmation classes, his father would take her to a motel), I want you to know what's been happening to him (he was on the run now), because you can become entangled with his situation without you knowing it, Antonio's mother said, because there's people who could benefit from you intervening (the fourteen-year-old daughter's therapist had also been Antonio's mother's therapist in Bogotá, so this therapist had emailed Antonio's mother asking to please call her because she needed help confirming the accusations against his father), no, I don't want to know, your sister would say, and that was my fear, Antonio, that by not supporting that fourteen-year-old girl (Antonio's stepsister), or the newborn (Antonio's half sister), that Estela or any one of us in the family might suffer repercussions, even your daughters, Antonio, so I would insist and she would refuse, to this day I can't talk to her about what's been happening with your father in Bogotá (even if Antonio landed in Bogotá, located his father wherever he was hiding (his aunt Elena, the Exorcist, knew where he was because Antonio contacted her before, when he was trying to talk to his father—I didn't do anything wrong that girl seduced me she was mature beyond her years, his father said—the first time I'd spoken to that man in twenty-one years—), and knifed him so he would cease to spread misery, the misery across generations, according to my mother's constellations, wouldn't end—how else will we make it end, Mother?—we must bring the perpetrator into the fold—no—), please, Antonio's mother said, there's an energetic entanglement due to what has been happening with your father, no, my daddy didn't do anything, my daddy this, my daddy that, as if to submerge that part of her pain, because she had too much already with what was happening to her in Baltimore, and so it came to a point where I told her yes, it happened, he wrote you a letter confessing and apologizing, and I read it, I couldn't remember, Mom, your sister said, I thought nothing had happened, and I think because your sister was in so much pain, she mixed everything up, blocking out what had happened to her so many years ago, enough, Antonio thinks, it's 9:01 a.m. already, time for SQL queries, proc means, nested where statements, so Antonio removes his oversized circumaural Sennheiser headphones, which have been transmitting his mother's voice for months, buries his sketchbook with the metadata of his recording of his mother under his Prudential Investments binders, runs his first batch of SQL queries, tries to read The Unnamable online, receives a call from his sister's attorney, who informs him his sister has at last agreed to a plea for three counts of disorderly misconduct, twelve months of outpatient treatment, twelve months of probation, and a commitment to leave the state of Maryland and never return—this has been one of the most rewarding cases of my career, his sister's attorney says, to see your sister recovering—runs his second and third batch of SQL queries, packs his sketchbook that contains the metadata of his recording of his mother, the metadata of his recording of his former wife, the notes he's been jotting down about his arrangements, about his sister, about the (so many) fictions that have been coursing through him for years (Antonio has been unable to write anything of consequence since summer #8, except the story of Dora and her dog, which contained no imaginative writing since it was an almost exact transcription of what Dora told him about her dog), switches off the fluorescence of his cubicle, rides his Shadow VLX to the apartment where his daughters live and where at last his former wife begins to speak to him, we need to talk, his former wife says, after the girls are asleep yes, Antonio says, Tata do Froggie Froggie, Eva says, not today, Antonio says, come on, Tata, Ada says, hey Froggie, Antonio says [in a severe voice], these girls want to talk to you come over here, what?, Antonio says [in an incredulous voice], you're busy eating fly soup? [Ada and Eva laugh], and so Antonio huffs away and Froggie appears and says [in a dumb country voice] hiiii you all doing, good, Ada and Eva say [pretending to be unamused], hey is that a fly cupcake, Froggie says, noooooo, Eva and Ada say, oh, gotta go, wait come back Froggie, Ada and Eva say [in mock alarm], have you seen Froggie Froggie, Antonio says [reappearing as himself], yeah he was just here, Eva says [as nonchalant as possible], huh, Antonio says, didn't see him, dinner's ready, Ida says, knock knock, Eva says, who's there, Antonio says, interrupting cow, Eva says, interrupting who, Antonio says, moo, Eva says, no you're supposed to interrupt him with your moo, Ada says, again, Eva says, time to brush your teeth, Ida says, bedtime, Ida says, I Had Trouble in Getting to Solla Sollew by Dr. Seuss, Antonio says, lights off, Ida says, one by one the lights were all extinguished, Virginia Woolf says, there's a nostalgic appeal to the asinine Frog skit, Antonio jots down on his sketchbook, because Eva and Ada and I have been sharing the asinine Frog skit with one another for almost three years, since the time they would take baths together, do you want to be with us, Ida says, yes, Antonio says, switching on the extractor above the stove so the girls can't hear them, do you want to continue being part of this family, Ida says, yes, Antonio says, we are not teenagers anymore, Ida says, I can't be running after you, keeping tabs on you, and I won't, Ida says, not anymore, but do know I have only so much patience left, Ida says, at some point I will just leave do you understand, Antonio says, and do know that if a butterfly were to land on my shoulder, Antonio doesn't say, I would burst from grief and say how will I ever repay you for everything you have given me, Ida, and thankfully Ida doesn't sit on the slate steps and doesn't explain to him, Antonio Jose Jiménez, patiently and for the thousandth time, that this was no longer his home (it still is), that the locks have been changed for this very reason (his keys still work), that he had to stop coming around here, upsetting her, upsetting the children, any news of your sister, Ida says, yes, Antonio says, pausing to compose himself (and show, with his composure, that what Ida has said has computed with him and that he is capable of complying), if all goes well my sister will be released tomorrow.

ESTELA JIMÉNEZ BY ANTONIO JOSE JIMÉNEZ

When did you start hearing voices, Antonio says, on a Sunday as I drove my mother to the airport my mother was there I'd become a bit paranoid of everything because Cristian had been conspiring against me always sharing my personal information with our coworkers at Fidelity Insurance so I'd ask my mother to come to Baltimore, and she came, and I didn't want her to leave that Sunday as I drove her to the airport that's when I realized there was this situation of voices I don't know if perhaps they started before, little by little or all of a sudden, but the first time I remember was a Sunday as I drove my mother to the airport later I developed insomnia due to what was happening, what was happening, Antonio says, the noises, the voices, I couldn't sleep, I would try to negotiate with them so they would go away some of the voices were independent from my logical self there's a part that's independent, and a part that's subjective that joins your thoughts the independent part says three or four things and then your subjective part fills the rest they're independent thoughts that you didn't think, they say, for instance, I want to shower this afternoon and you didn't think this but the thought was there, independent, almost everything was related to my job the voices were voices from people at Fidelity Insurance, so the first time you heard voices you heard the voices of your coworkers, Antonio says, yes I drove to work what transpired was a negotiation every day trying to negotiate for these voices to leave they wouldn't leave I would drive to the gym and everything it began to escalate because I continued to negotiate and they wouldn't leave that anxiety that they wouldn't leave, that they would stay permanently, that fear began to escalate until I ended up driving to the hospital because I couldn't sleep, that was the first time at the emergency room when you couldn't sleep, Antonio says, the fear becomes part of your thoughts you can't control them you live in a cloud of independent thoughts that you can't control, what would they say to you, Antonio says, I don't remember at some point I wrote them down they were persecutory they would reject me I do remember that during my leave of absence at work I would remain in bed negotiating trying to exit this cloud of thoughts they would tell me we are the, we are the, how does it go, not the incorruptibles, like a group that demands a lot, the untouchables, Antonio says, no, there's a word, I can't remember, like a group that's severe with you that is not going to forgive you I returned to work hearing voices they never went away it's only recently sleeping over at my Mom's house in Sioux Falls that they've been gone completely, when you came here to Los Angeles for that one weekend were you already hearing voices, Antonio says, yes I think I told you the doctor in the hospital told me that it happens to a lot of people these independent thoughts are so intelligent that you think how is it that this can be I used to compare it to a noise coming from an earpiece the doctor said many people think they are being recruited by the government what happens is that you can't believe that this is happening to you did you see the movie A Beautiful Mind, yes, Antonio says, the protagonist thought he was being recruited by the government too in the hospital it wasn't just about voices but about memories, because my memory started to fail me, certain memories that I had that now that I am rested I know aren't true when I was in jail I was convinced that a former boyfriend who was in real estate wanted my house so he plotted with those people who called the police on me the doctor said that that was unlikely the doctor tried to remove me from that cloud that I was in I

was surprised by it sometimes it scares me because I only realized it later how can it be that these nebulous memories that
aren't true have filtered through, later I had hallucinations in
my house I was having them the day I was arrested I'd been
having hallucinations for like two days about my neighbor
crossing my front door like a ghost these are symptoms of the
same sickness, the doctor said, in the hospital they ask you as
part of the questionnaire if you have auditory problems, visual
problems, in jail it happened that I had a lot of hallucinations,
in the hospital as well I was in a solitary cell for too long I don't
know if part of the brain becomes agitated something happens
to it it starts to produce hallucinations because when I was in
the hospital it was the opposite I was always relating to others
so the hallucinations went away as if my brain couldn't produce
them anymore when I was younger I could be alone and face
anything but my brain didn't produce these kinds of hallucinations now it seems that with age, whenever I'm alone, isolated,
my brain, dinner's ready, Ida says, we're recording give us a
minute, Antonio says, now or never, monkeys, Ida says, I'm
hungry, Toñito, Estela says, and so Antonio pauses the recording
and Estela and Antonio join their mother, Ida, Ada, and Eva at
the dinner table, tell us the one about how Mama and Tata met,
Tata, Ada says, don't mind them it's a game they play, Ida says,
a game that consists of Antonio inventing scenarios of how Antonio and Ida met, when Mama and Tata first met, Antonio says,
Mama was selling mangoes on the side of the road, why mangoes, Tata, Eva says, and I came into her mango stand, her face
as red as a lobster, and I asked her where the closest gas station
was because I had to pee and guess what she said, whut?, Ada
and Eva say, that's right, Antonio says, whut, they're making
fun of me I don't say whut like that, Ida says, never, Antonio says,
but of course there had been no mango stand or gas station,

only a sky cabin in Tahoe where, on the bottom floor, while he was reading a paperback of Catch-22 instead of drinking with the repulsive investment bankers above (Antonio had agreed to the Tahoe trip because his friend Nicole wanted him to see snow), he saw Ida for the first time, ambling as if in penance because earlier she'd forgotten the sunblock so her face was as red as a lobster, and although he doesn't remember what he said to her, or what she said to him, he remembers telling his friend Nicole as soon as she breaks up with that retrograde investment banker you call me, a call that arrived a year later, on a Tuesday—we're at Taco Tuesdays, Nicole said, she's here and she's very single—and she was so striking, this Amazon woman from Eastern Europe, as his mother called her upon meeting her for the first time, jumping around in her suede cowboy boots and her cowboy hat because she was free of the burden of boyfriend and all she wanted to do was dance, and all every man wanted to do was dance with her, including Antonio, of course, and so Antonio and Ida did (just as friends though due to Ida wanting to be free of boyfriends), two or three times a week (in all the photos from those days, which Antonio keeps in his file cabinet inside his cubicle, Antonio and Ida look drunk, Antonio grinning at the camera while Ida's holding a bottle of champagne like a newborn, for instance), until one Sunday afternoon, at a street party, where a Spaniard had been about to succeed in seducing Ida—she's a bit nuts, Antonio said to the Spaniard, I would avoid her if I were you—Ida said I'm horny, and Antonio said that's what friends are for, and so he flagged a cab for them—so glad there was no cameras in that cab, Ida has said over the years—how do you know there weren't any, eh?—and when they arrived at her apartment she said to her roommates, who were watching television, let's order pizza, as if to cover for what they were about to do, which they did, that day and the next day and the next, for almost two years electrifying each other before parties, after parties, at his apartment that soon became her apartment—we never did order that pizza, Ida has said over the years—let's order it now—stopping on their way to Sonoma, midway, so they could do it again at a two-star hotel, where the maid walked in on them and stayed two or three seconds too long before saying excuse me—we never made it to Sonoma, Tato—and one day it was over, as it always had been for Antonio, or so he thought, because on the Sunday she was about to move out, he, for practical reasons (she was flying to Czechia in a few weeks anyway so why not wait until she left to break up?—not for practical reasons, Antonio's mother said, you just didn't want her to go—if you would have broken up with me while I was in Czechia that summer I wouldn't have come back, Antonio—but you never made it to Czechia because we conceived Ada—), changed his mind, covering the walls of their apartment with Post-it notes that said please don't go, please stay, and so she did.

—

What else do you want to know, Toñito, no but without the iPad, Antonio says, but it's boring otherwise, come now, Antonio says, nooooo [in a child's voice], put away the iPad please, Antonio says, hmmmpff, okay let's restart, seeing those ghosts must have been scary, Antonio says, I'm still scared there's a possibility I will get deported I would say my god what's going to happen even my uncle Francisco would cross my front door as a ghost I was watching a lot of television because the television was always on at a high volume and they would show movies what we used to do at the hospital is play cards and watch television or walk through the hallways if we watched a good movie that would be our only connection with the exterior world I remember watching The Hunger Games the man from Hunger Games the one who plays President Snow I would see him entering my cell like a ghost that is not a ghost that's a hallucination in the cell in the hospital as well, when you were in jail you were alone, Antonio says, yes for a little while I shared a cell with someone but most of the time I was alone I became scared you can waste a whole day looking at these ghosts a woman in my cell would tell me we're going to have a secret you talk to yourself I won't tell anybody because the process of transferring me from jail to the hospital lasted so long there was no connection with anyone you saw what the phones were like sometimes I would spend most of the day writing letters I wrote letters to the judge that's probably why they transferred me to the hospital I wrote that my mother had injected me, that you had participated, that the two of you had kidnapped me they realized this was improbable they became concerned at first my lawyer wasn't sure do you want to talk to your family or not, he said, when I began to regain my reason I said yes after I was arrested the first time the hallucinations went away they returned on my birthday a year later they were horrible I think it was because I was scared I would get deported back to Colombia and I would have to see Antonio Senior again I get along with our cousin Isabel over the internet my Mom has received messages from Aunt Elena that sometimes I'm like how is it possible that they're still defending him you can come and stay with us, Isabel said, our family is very close, but Isabel is still Aunt Elena's daughter, they are still his sisters and nieces no matter how much they offer to help it's strange I know it isn't their fault because of the possibility of deportation a terror visited me the possibility of separation of our family how will I deal with that family over there, so a year after your first arrest you became scared of deportation, Antonio says, it was as if ghosts were attacking me, what do you think prompted it, Antonio says, because I wasn't getting along with you or my Mom I was living in an environment in which Cristian rallied our coworkers against me they lied and said I had complained of harassment which wasn't true he acted like the victim obviously I have a problem that if I neglect rest or healthy eating it's possible this sickness will return I stopped taking sleeping pills the doctor doesn't think the sleeping pills caused the hallucinations I came to realize that at my Mom's house by resting a lot they went away I still have that strange sound, which I've looked for on the internet, there is a sickness, I wrote down the symptoms, the name, white noise in the brain, I think, most of the time it doesn't bother me when I lie down to sleep the brain feels more pressure when I'm walking not as much either way I've become nervous because it makes me feel more predisposed to death there's a word for that, not more human, vulnerable, Antonio says, I don't remember, yes, more predisposed to death, because it's an imbalance of the body, the body begins to get sick is it a symptom of something else is it going to be the case that I will have to leave this world at a young age remember we had that problem with our teeth are these signs that genetically our body isn't going to last like other people who die of cancer when they're forty or fifty that's what I think about here in Los Angeles I have to constantly eat fruit because I feel my blood pressure dropping if I don't eat a certain amount my energy levels don't rise these downswings are too large are they part of some sickness my Mom doesn't hear any noises she doesn't have these downswings it does worry me, Toñito.

—

Tell me about Milwaukee, Antonio says, I was conscious that
the moment that they arrest you for what they arrested me for,
first of all a terrible depression came over me, because I'd been
charged with five felonies, so that's enough for me not to be able
to work ever again in insurance to only be able to work at a
Wendy's or Burger King, places like that, because those charges
show up in background checks now I have three counts of disorderly conduct all the same they won't hire you, I'm not working now because it's too tiring though I was working in an office
after the arrest I had to do these drug tests, exams, I had a problem at work I began to think I was going to end up in jail the
lawyer never told me that there's usually a plea agreement I was
up in the air, scared, I don't know if the lawyers do it to make
you beg, I'm not going to end up in jail, I said to myself, I have
savings, I had saved something like fifty thousand dollars, and
I am going to spend my savings, and I am going to see the world,
and I've spent all these years working so hard to end up with
these charges, and I am going to end up in jail who knows for
how many years, so I started to travel I drove to Milwaukee, I
removed all my belongings from my house later they auctioned
them all away because I didn't pay the storage fees, and so I
drove to Montana multiple times, what did you do in Montana,
Antonio says, drive around, stay in hotels I spent all my credit,
the fifty thousand plus all my credit lines, so when you arrived
to Milwaukee you didn't have any money anymore, Antonio
says, yes I was already low on money toward the end before they
apprehended me I sold my car, I didn't have any money, any gas,
I went to a CarMax and sold my car for two thousand dollars
then they arrested me I was having memory problems I was at a
laundromat, oh, okay, I was sleeping in an immense shelter but
I discovered that I could sleep by the side of the, I became a

member of a gym I would shower there at night I would sleep
next to the storage because it was in a basement I slept better
there than in a shelter there was a woman who had gone there
to sleep too no one said anything it was all bulletproof with
cameras and everything I made a little bed next to it I would
wake up early I would walk, I started watching movies, at some
point I developed this idea that I'd met Brad Pitt when I was
young, strange things were happening to my memory, because
of what you had done to commit me in the hospital I thought
you and Ida were against me so when they called the police at
the laundromat I think I had called a man a Nazi, you're a Nazi,
I said, they paid you, and you and Ida were Nazis as well who
had paid this man to block my way in the laundromat the atten-
dants called the police due to a disturbance the police arrived
to check what was happening but there were no charges or anything when they scanned my license I don't know I guess they
saw I had a warrant these kinds of hallucinations were already
happening to me I was sure you had followed me to Milwaukee
I'd seen a girl who looked just like Ida on the train, Ida is following me, I would think, or I would see someone who looked
like you from behind my brother is following me they're going
to intern me you are Nazis, so I think it was many years of living
with so much pressure, of not living close to family, plus the situation with Cristian exacerbated it as he conspired with others
at work against me, since we didn't have a more peaceful relationship, or with more people around, so it developed into para-
noia I was surprised my memories were so affected I don't know
why like I said they are symptoms of a sickness the doctor said
there are people who think they are being recruited by the government and that happened to me too I began to research government spying capabilities I even shared some printouts with
you because the independent voices were so intelligent that

one begins to fight against it or a part of you says this can't be so you begin to make up that you're being recruited because you can't believe that this is happening to you you live a life so full of discipline, being the best candidate in most of the jobs you apply for, and all of a sudden you can't control your thoughts, so you start to think you're being recruited because you can't believe it's happening to you I imagine that's what happened to that man, who died already, you can't believe it, which man, Antonio says, the one from A Beautiful Mind, what do you remember about us as siblings, Antonio says, I remember we used to play a lot until we were ten or so you grew up, started school at San Luis Gonzaga, and after that we didn't play anymore, how about before then, Antonio says, we would play house don't you remember we would make houses in our beds in our room in that house in Mirandela you had your bed I had mine I had a whole set with dolls we would join them with a bridge between the two beds we had a village on each side you had your own village on your side we would spend the whole day playing house, under the table, later they bought me ceramic jewelry from Bucaramanga and we would play with the jewelry then you grew up you would play Barbies with me and you would undress them and I would become upset because that's all you would do, undress them, I think I stopped playing with Barbies when I was ten because I was tired of you undressing them, I think you told me that even though you were hearing voices you could function and drive to Montana and Milwaukee what was that like, Antonio says, I would spend most of my time talking to myself, like answering, I don't remember what I was saying, I even considered driving to Los Angeles but the involuntary confinement had already happened but I would say I'll do it for my nieces, but you and Ida might call the police I don't want to be interned again, no, I would spend most of my time talking to myself because the voices were really strong and I wasn't sleeping well, to overcome this, to me it's a miracle, I mean when I walk, when I am walking around now here in Los Angeles and I don't hear anything except the external sounds I'm like whoa, but back then no, I was hearing voices and it was a nuisance, so to not hear them I would talk to myself, so there were different planes of reality, Antonio says, I think I drove to Montana because when I was young I had a good time there, when, Antonio says, when I was twenty-one with a boyfriend named Jonathan we went rafting, but I drove there in winter I began to think I'd gone to college there in winter with snow and he was there with me it was quite a mix-up my first lawyer had become upset had placed a restraining order on me he tried to negotiate so he wouldn't have to do it I had written him like five pages in my memory I was convinced that I had met him in college so in front of the judge I said I knew him from college and I was well-dressed, looked normal, but that wasn't true, when I was in jail I wrote a letter to his associate who had helped me before I apologized and told him I didn't know these were symptoms of a sickness when I was driving in Montana I thought I'd been in Montana with him, with Ronald Reagan and his wife and Amber, this girl from college, I think my mind produced these things I didn't know this wasn't true I would drive while it was snowing I think I crisscrossed Montana twice, and you would stay in hotels, Antonio says, yes but I would spend most of the day driving, and that helped you, Antonio says, because of the charges I couldn't stay calm what do you do when you have these kinds of charges and you think you are going to end up in jail so I spent most of my time driving around as if on holiday a part of me thought perhaps I wouldn't have been this way but I had worked so much, so hard, and life slips away, mortal, I think that's the word I was looking for, when you know that either way you're going to die, look at my uncle Patricio who used to drink, used to get drunk every day, he died when he was eighty-seven years old just like my grandmother who didn't drink, and one takes care of oneself, doesn't drink, doesn't get drunk, and yet ends up with this sickness, without eating pork, or any of those greasy things they used to eat, and life does slip away, Toñito, Tía Estela come read to me, Eva says, we're recording maybe later, Antonio says, Perro, Estela says, don't pet him or he'll pee on the bed, Eva says, our Eva looks just like our Estela doesn't she, Antonio's mother says, go read to them it's late they have school tomorrow, Ida says, milk in the batter, Antonio says, we bake cake, Eva says, and nothing's the matter, Ada says, say mnemocartography, Antonio says, if you go flying on a flying trapeze, Ada says, I will be a tightrope walker and walk across the air to you, Antonio says, quick, Tía Estela, Eva says, before lights-out.

Mauro Javier Cárdenas was born and brought up in Guayaquil, Ecuador, and studied Economics at Stanford University. His debut novel, *The Revolutionaries Try Again*, was published in 2016. He was awarded the 2016 Joseph Henry Jackson Award and was included in the Hay Festival anthology *Bogotá 39: New Voices from Latin America* (Oneworld, 2018), a selection of the best young Latin American novelists working today.